SGT PEPPER

AT FIFTY

THE MOOD, THE LOOK, THE SOUND, THE LEGACY
OF THE BEATLES' GREAT MASTERPIECE

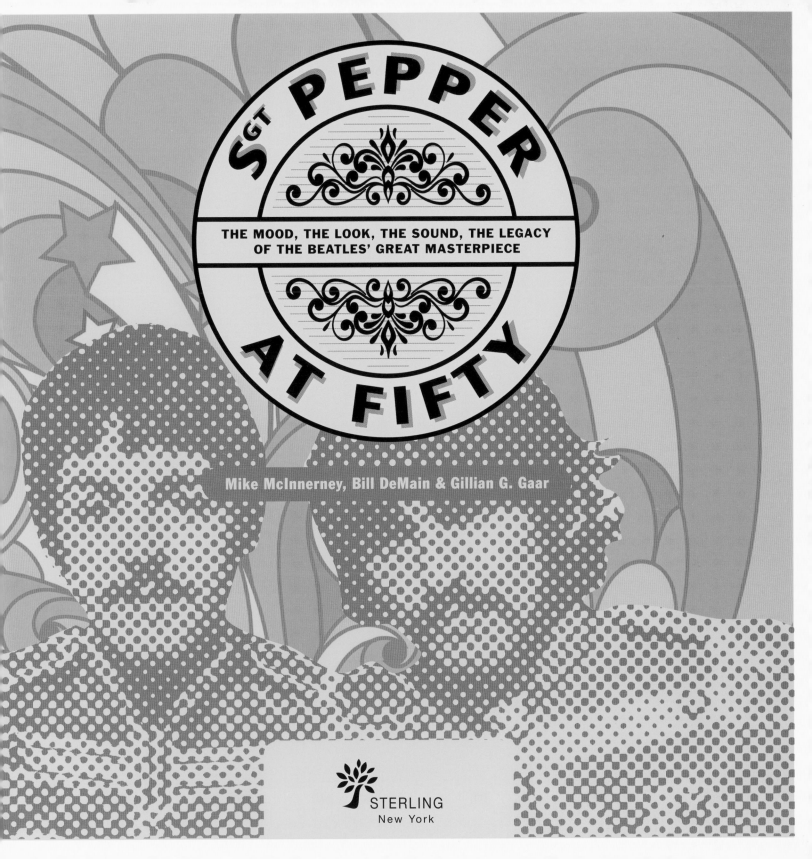

SGT PEPPER

THE MOOD, THE LOOK, THE SOUND, THE LEGACY
OF THE BEATLES' GREAT MASTERPIECE

AT FIFTY

Mike McInnerney, Bill DeMain & Gillian G. Gaar

STERLING
New York

STERLING
New York

An Imprint of Sterling Publishing Co., Inc.
1166 Avenue of the Americas
New York, NY 10016

ISBN 978-1-4549-2378-7

Distributed in Canada by Sterling Publishing Co., Inc.
c/o Canadian Manda Group, 664 Annette Street
Toronto, Ontario, Canada M6S 2C8

For information about custom editions, special sales,
and premium and corporate purchases, please contact Sterling
Special Sales at 800-805-5489 or specialsales@sterlingpublishing.com.

Manufactured in China

2 4 6 8 10 9 7 5 3 1

www.sterlingpublishing.com

Designed by Paul Palmer-Edwards

CONTENTS

Foreword

By Spencer Leigh

MY EXPECTATIONS WEREN'T HIGH when I went to see the 2016 film about the Beatles on tour, *Eight Days a Week*, but I am relieved to say that not only did the director, Ron Howard, preserve their heritage, he also brought something new to the table.

Previously, I had thought that George Harrison was the party pooper: the one who didn't want to tour anymore, and was fed up with being a Beatle. Now I understand why. Those stadium gigs in America were horrendous: the Beatles were playing in sports venues using crummy PAs, and the fans were often penned in behind barriers. The sheer intensity of their passion for the Beatles could easily have triggered a major tragedy, so the band and their fans were lucky to come out unscathed.

The Beatles could hardly hear each other as they went through the motions onstage, and away from the fans they were treated with little respect. The film news footage of them rolling around in an empty security van as they are driven away at speed from a stadium would make anyone glad not to be a Beatle.

After the Candlestick Park gig in 1966, George got on the plane and said, "Well, that's it, I'm not a Beatle anymore." Of course he was still a Beatle, but apart from TV appearances and that famous performance up on the roof of Apple Corps. in 1969, the band never played in public again.

These days, albums are little more than promos for tours and that is where the bands make their money. Not in 1967. The Beatles maintained that *Sgt. Pepper's Lonely Hearts Club Band* was a studio album, and that it would be impossible to replicate it onstage.

I suspect that this was an excuse— today, even pub bands can perform a reasonable facsimile of the work. Perhaps the technology wasn't fully there in 1967, but surely they could have devised a way of presenting this material onstage, especially with George Martin's assistance? After all, they were the Beatles. The evidence, I think, is plain: it wasn't that they couldn't do it; they didn't *want* to do it.

A few months ago, I was talking to Gary Brooker about Procol Harum's "A Whiter Shade of Pale," which is among the most enduring records from the Summer of Love. He said, "We were not following a trend, as when we made that record, we were in advance of it. 'A Whiter Shade of Pale' was recorded in April, and a lot of the other key records were made around that time. So it was really the Spring of Love, and to me the Summer of Love is an artistic pipedream."

Perhaps Gary is right. The Beatles made *Sgt. Pepper* in the winter, and had been working on songs for the animated cartoon *Yellow Submarine* and others that wound up in *Magical Mystery Tour* before the album was even released.

Sgt. Pepper at Fifty looks at the creation of the Beatles' landmark album from four different angles, each covered in a separate chapter: the Mood, the Look, the Sound, and the Legacy.

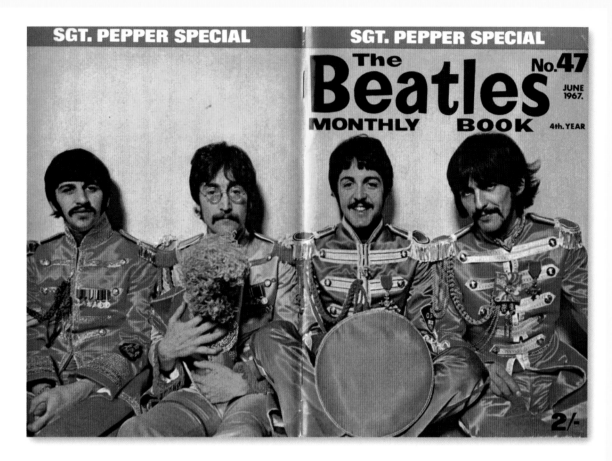

SGT. PEPPER SPECIAL

The Beatles MONTHLY BOOK No.47 JUNE 1967. 4th. YEAR 2/-

RIGHT: The June 1967 issue of *The Beatles Monthly Book* was devoted entirely to the band's new album, with the wraparound cover unveiling their new look.

I enjoyed Mike McInnerney's theme of setting out the mood for *Sgt. Pepper*. I love all this early sixties history. Back then, I had heard of the International Poetry Incarnation at the Royal Albert Hall through Peter Whitehead's film *Wholly Communion*, but all of the background to all this counterculture is fascinating—particularly when it is written by someone who was there, taking his own trips. Mike can both remember the sixties and was there.

Bill DeMain is a fine rock journalist, known for asking searching questions of great songwriters, and here he handles the look of *Sgt. Pepper*, deftly analyzing how the cover art came into being. The Beatles always had "the look." They look great in any picture, no matter what they are wearing. They always look like a group. By way of contrast, look at the Byrds: they invariably look like a bunch of disparate (not to mention desperate) young men.

There had been concept albums before the Beatles, but there had been nothing so lavish and extravagant before. I can recall buying the album at NEMS in Liverpool and being surprised that it was still being sold at the standard price for an LP.

Pepper seemed to have everything: an extraordinary variety of songs on all manner of subjects, from parking meters and circus posters to tripping and retirement; the lyrics printed on the

sleeve, itself a rarity; the Pop Art cutouts; and, most of all, that extraordinary cover, which has been copied and parodied to this day. (The only one Sir Peter Blake doesn't like is Frank Zappa's *We're Only in It for the Money*, but I think the latter is an affectionate parody, even if Sir Peter doesn't.)

As Gillian G. Gaar points out, *Sgt. Pepper*'s legacy is enduring. It changed popular music in a way that could never have been envisaged. Soon, every man and his dog were releasing concept albums—some excellent (the Moody Blues, the Who, the Pretty Things, the Kinks), some in my view deplorable (the Rolling Stones' *Their Satanic Majesties Request*). We now know how good the Beach Boys' *Smile* would have been, too, but at the time they just gave up.

Sadly, the Beatles' message of "love, love, love" didn't change the world, but they certainly did a lot of good. As Leslie Woodhead argues in *How the Beatles Rocked the Kremlin*, they played an effective role in demolishing the Iron Curtain. I live in Liverpool, and every time I am in the city center, I am surrounded by all nationalities, including Russians. These four young men helped to make it happen.

Both Mark Lewisohn and Jon Savage have told me that the Beatles' records sound different when you are high. I have never been high, but I will bear it in mind for when I am about to shuffle off. I will ask my wife to go to the railroad bridge for a toke or two. I shall put the records on (vinyl, please) and wait for the newspaper taxi to take me away . . .

Spencer Leigh
Liverpool, England
October 2016

OPPOSITE: Fans invade the field during the Beatles' final concert, Candlestick Park, San Francisco, August 29, 1966.

RIGHT: A poster for the Candlestick Park show.

BELOW: Tickets for the band's performances in San Francisco and at New York's Shea Stadium the previous weekend.

Introduction

By Gillian G. Gaar

THE BEATLES WHO SET ABOUT MAKING *SGT. PEPPER* were four young men at the peak of their musical powers and creative curiosity, exploring and assimilating everything from the sitar and self-realization to countercultural art and all-night happenings. The result was a distillation of all these ideas and more: an art-pop masterwork housed in a gatefold Pop Art masterpiece.

It's ironic that a groundbreaking album that took rock to such unimagined new heights begins with a line referencing the past. For when the Beatles (or, to be more precise, Paul McCartney) opened *Sgt. Pepper's Lonely Hearts Club Band* by informing the listener that the good sergeant's band had got its start "twenty years ago today," the Beatles were regarded as the most up-to-date and au courant rock act of the era—at the forefront of every developing trend, the first to sight the distant shores of the next big thing. "The Beatles were in the crow's nest, shouting 'Land ho!,'" as John Lennon put it in one of his last interviews, with *Playboy*, in 1980.

Or maybe it wasn't so strange. The Beatles were great synthesizers. They drew from their collective past and built on it, combining American rock 'n' roll and British music hall and fashioning a new kind of music that felt different, fresh, and exciting.

It's been said that the arrival of the Beatles took rock 'n' roll out its post-fifties slump, when the genre's original innovators—Elvis Presley, Chuck Berry, Buddy Holly, Little Richard—had fallen by the wayside, replaced by such anodyne pop crooners as Frankie Avalon, James Darren, and a plethora of Bobbys (Bobby Rydell, Bobby Vee, Bobby Darin, Bobby Vinton). In fact, it wasn't quite that dreary. The years between 1958 (when Presley entered the army and Berry and Richard had their last big hits) and 1962 (when the Beatles released their first single, "Love Me Do"), saw the emergence of numerous innovative performers, including Ray Charles (whose crossover hit, "What'd I Say," came in 1959), the Beach Boys (who released their first record in 1961), and Bob Dylan (who released his first record in 1962). In 1959, the Detroit-based Motown Records put out the first release on its subsidiary label Tamla;

the company would release numerous records that were a huge influence on the Beatles, including "Money (That's What I Want)," "Please Mr. Postman," and "You've Really Got a Hold on Me," all of which they covered; they also regularly expressed their admiration for other Motown acts like Marvin Gaye. It was also the era of the girl groups—acts like the Shirelles, the Crystals, and the Chiffons; groups whose melodic, soulful songs of heartbreak and teenage angst had a vibrant authenticity (and whom the Beatles also admired).

Nonetheless, there was no rock act that hit the collective pop-culture consciousness with the seismic force of a Presley during those years. And then came the Beatles. Their astonishing success in the UK in 1963 was like nothing Britain had ever seen. And in addition to their commercial success, interest in the group attracted more than just the teen set.

RIGHT: The fresh-faced Fab Four at Alpha TV Studios in Birmingham, England, during filming of the ABC-TV show *Lucky Stars*, August 18, 1963.

"People of all ages and all intellects had succumbed," Hunter Davies wrote in his authorized biography of the band. Just one year prior, the Beatles had been slogging it out through another extended run at the Star Club in Hamburg, Germany, playing sets that were largely comprised of cover songs like "Be-Bop-a-Lula," "Sweet Little Sixteen," "To Know Her Is to Love Her," and "I'm Gonna Sit Right Down and Cry (Over You)." Now, as 1963 came to a close, the London *Times* hailed Lennon and McCartney as "the outstanding English composers of 1963," while the *Sunday Times* called them "the greatest composers since Beethoven." The response in the US in 1964 was just as

enthusiastic. One week, *The Singing Nun* was in its tenth week at the top of the *Billboard* album charts; the next week, *Meet the Beatles!* began its eleven-week reign there, replaced by *The Beatles' Second Album* in May, which remained at No. 1 for five weeks. *A Hard Day's Night* was the No. 1 album for fourteen weeks, which meant the Beatles were top of the pops for a record-breaking thirty weeks in 1964.

Nor was that the only record smashed that year. Over 73 million people watched the Beatles make their live TV debut in the US on *The Ed Sullivan Show* on February 9—the largest ever viewing audience at the time. And on April 4, the Beatles held the top five spots in

> **ONE REASON WE DON'T WANT TO TOUR ANYMORE IS THAT WHEN WE'RE ONSTAGE NOBODY CAN HEAR US OR LISTEN TO US. AND ANOTHER REASON IS THAT OUR STAGE ACT HASN'T IMPROVED ONE BIT SINCE WE STARTED TOURING FOUR YEARS AGO."** Paul McCartney, 1967

Billboard's pop singles chart, a feat unlikely to be repeated (that same week, *Meet the Beatles!* was still at No. 1, and *Introducing . . . the Beatles* was at No. 2). The Beatles truly were, as they'd once

OPPOSITE, FAR LEFT: The Beatles pose in front of animated versions of themselves in London, November 11, 1964.

OPPOSITE, LEFT: On *Rubber Soul* (1965), the Beatles moved beyond the "boy-meets-girl" themes of their early material into more mature, experimental territory.

ABOVE: By the time of *Revolver* (1966), the studio itself became an increasingly integral component of the Beatles' sound.

ABOVE RIGHT: Beatles fans at Shea Stadium, New York, August 23, 1966.

joked in a pep talk they'd give themselves before they landed a record deal, "the toppermost of the poppermost."

But where would they go from here? No rock act had, as yet, successfully risen from teen-idol stardom to being a serious artist. Conventional wisdom for a pop star was to cash in while you could, then transition into more mainstream "light" entertainment, like variety shows and films. In Britain, Tommy Steele had taken this path, with great success. But there were also risks. Elvis Presley had left behind his wild Hillbilly Cat persona when he was discharged from the army in 1960, wasting most of the decade by appearing in an increasingly undistinguished series of movies, stuck performing execrable songs like "There's No Room to Rhumba in a Sports Car" and "Yoga Is as Yoga Does." The films might have been profitable, but the commercial success came at the expense of his artistic integrity.

The Beatles would not make the same mistake. They were determined to not repeat themselves; every time they went in to make a new record, their prime objective was to make it different from the previous one. And as the band members matured, so did their music. By the time of *Rubber Soul* (1965), they'd moved beyond simple boy-meets-girl tunes like "From Me to You." There was even a track on *Rubber Soul*

> **" WHAT THIS GANG OF PEOPLE FROM THE *INTERNATIONAL TIMES*, INDICA, AND THE WHOLE SCENE IS TRYING TO DO IS TRY TO SEE WHERE WE ARE NOW AND SEE WHAT WE'VE GOT AROUND US; SEE ANY MISTAKES WE'VE MADE AND STRAIGHTEN 'EM OUT."** Paul McCartney, 1967

that wasn't a love song at all, "Nowhere Man," an early slice of social commentary from Lennon. The band's next UK single, "Paperback Writer" / "Rain," was their first 45 where neither side addressed the subject of romance.

The group was also keenly attuned to the cultural developments around them, and by the mid-sixties, London was a very exciting place to be. The success of the Beatles helped establish the idea that for a rock band to have any credibility, they had to write their own songs. It was something that would influence every subsequent rock act, regardless of their musical similarity to the Beatles. Suddenly, there were numerous groups performing original material: the Rolling Stones, the Kinks, the Who, the Byrds, Jefferson Airplane, Jimi Hendrix, and more, all of whom, along with the Beach Boys and Bob Dylan, helped "rock 'n' roll" mature into "rock."

In London, there was an artistic cross-fertilization across disciplines as well, with musicians rubbing elbows with painters, filmmakers, poets, actors, writers, photographers, and playwrights. As a teenager, future Beatles manager Brian Epstein had horrified his father when he announced he wanted to be a dress designer (he was soon safely ensconced learning the family business in one of his father's furniture shops). Now Britain's own Mary Quant was revolutionizing the fashion industry with her designs, neatly erasing the stereotype of a perennially tweed-clad Britain with her miniskirts and what she called "easy, youthful, simple clothes, in which you could move." After years of following America's lead, London—in particular during the era of "Swinging London"—had become the most trendsetting place on earth.

> **" PEOPLE ARE VERY, VERY AWARE OF WHAT'S GOING ON AROUND THEM NOWADAYS. THEY THINK FOR THEMSELVES, AND I DON'T THINK WE CAN EVER BE ACCUSED OF UNDER-ESTIMATING THE INTELLIGENCE OF OUR FANS."** George Harrison, 1967

The Beatles absorbed all of these influences in every aspect of their work. They put as much thought into the design of their record covers as they did their music. Fans copied their tastes in fashion (Cuban-heeled boots, jackets with velvet collars) as much as their tastes in musical instruments (Rickenbacker guitars, Hofner violin basses). And their interest in remaining ahead of the curve musically was leading them to experiment as never before in the studio. How the music was recorded became increasingly important; the sonic experimentation on *Revolver* (1966) and the last songs the band recorded in 1966 ("Strawberry Fields Forever" and "Penny Lane," released as a single in early 1967), took them into a dazzling new music realm, of which *Sgt. Pepper's Lonely Hearts Club Band* was the apotheosis.

Sgt. Pepper was the Beatles' State of the Union address for 1967. But it also reflected the state of the world as much as the band's own state of mind. The Beatles, England, and the world had undergone many changes in the five years since the band had released their first record. As the cover made clear, the world was a more colorful place. The title song celebrated the past, but there was an optimistic outlook for the future as well ("Getting Better"). It was a world of vivid daydreams ("Lucy in the Sky with Diamonds"), and taking comfort in getting by "With a Little Help from My Friends." But it was also a more complicated world, with the album's songs addressing the generation gap ("She's Leaving Home"), the boredom of day-to-day modern life ("Good Morning, Good Morning"), and existential angst ("A Day in the Life").

In short, it was an album dealing with life's joys, sorrows, and anxieties. It was an aural depiction of Swinging London at its sparkling height. The Beatles drew on the myriad influences around them, and created something uniquely their own. It was hailed as the greatest album of all time on the day it was released. And though that assessment has been challenged in the years since, for many it still holds true. One thing is certain: people will still be listening to, talking about, and debating the merits of *Sgt. Pepper* for years to come.

Welcome to *Sgt. Pepper*: the mood, the look, the sound, and the legacy.

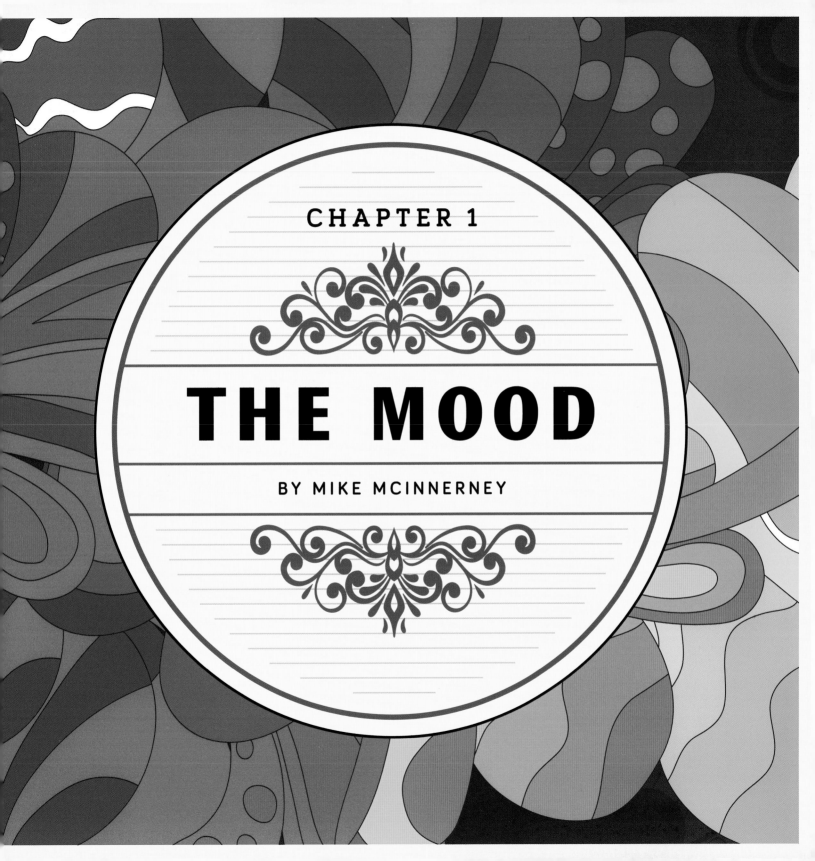

"The thing the sixties did was to show us the possibilities and the responsibility that we all had. It wasn't the answer. It just gave us a glimpse of the possibility."

John Lennon to RKO Radio, December 8, 1980

AT THE TIME OF THE BEATLES' HAMBURG DEBUT in 1960, Britain was changing rapidly. The invasion of Egypt, and the resulting "Suez Crisis" of 1956, had exposed Britain's weakness as a military power to the world; in 1960, at the end of a visit to British colonies in Africa, Prime Minister Harold Macmillan effectively announced the final dismantling of the British Empire in his famous "wind[s] of change" speech.

Things were changing at home, too. A "New Left"—a broad range of protest and activist movements, such as the Campaign for Nuclear Disarmament, or CND, formed in 1957—had grown out of the Suez Crisis and the 1956 Soviet invasion of Hungary. And there was a new cultural energy in the air. Driven by frustration with the complacency of the old social order, much of this energy focused on describing the frustrations and limitations of life for working-class characters in modern Britain, or for those "misfits" who'd found no place in traditional, class-bound Britain. This was expressed in literature, in movies, and on TV. Movies such as *Saturday Night and Sunday Morning* (1960), an adaptation of Alan Sillitoe's 1956 novel, and John Osborne's play *Look Back in Anger* (1956) both featured blue-collar "Angry Young Men" (as the critics named them), and both were from the "provinces"—that is, not from London. In the meantime, the first episode of a gritty Northern soap opera called *Coronation Street*, set in Manchester and created by Manchester-based Granada TV, was first broadcast in 1960. Also in 1960, Harold Pinter's play *The Caretaker*, about the power struggles between a tramp, a disabled handyman, and his brother, premiered at London's Arts Theatre Club, changing the face of modern theatre, and Lynne Reid Banks's novel *The L-Shaped Room* (1960), again

PREVIOUS SPREAD: Two young hippies relax beside the fountains in Trafalgar Square, London, summer 1967.

OPPOSITE, RIGHT: British prime minister Harold Macmillan and US president John F. Kennedy attend a press conference together in Washington, D.C., April 29, 1962.

OPPOSITE, FAR RIGHT: New British prime minister Harold Wilson (*center*) and his wife, Mary, meet Kennedy's successor, Lyndon B. Johnson, at the White House, March 2, 1964.

about outsiders and misfits, was an instant success.

In national political terms, prime minster Macmillan, clearly sensing that the winds of change were sweeping Britain, too, ended conscription to the British army (the last man was called up for National Service in 1963), but the Vassall and Profumo scandals (first, in 1961, British civil servant John Vassall was found to have been spying for the Soviet Union; then, in 1963, Secretary of State for War John Profumo admitted to having had a relationship, in 1961, with the nineteen-year-old Christine Keeler, while she was involved with the USSR naval attaché in London) cast a miasma of corruption and moral decay over Macmillan, his government, and the British establishment. New Labour Party opposition leader Harold Wilson promised voters a revolution if he and his party were elected, and spoke of "the Britain that is going to be forged in the

white heat of this revolution." Wilson was elected prime minister in 1964.

The events of the sixties (and of the seventies and eighties), meanwhile, were to be played out against the background of the Cold War, and the continuing threat of nuclear war—a threat vividly brought to life by 1962's face-off between the US and the USSR, during the Cuban Missile Crisis. But the Angry Young Men—and Women—of the postwar generation were truly coming of age in this new decade. Determined to test the tired establishment rules of behavior, the young began to challenge established assumptions with a high degree of hope in their own future—a future that would include peace, love, and a belief in goodness and beauty. Established ideas about class identity were challenged more widely, too. Previous generations had often attempted to adopt the style and manners of the upper classes as they

> **WE STAND TODAY ON THE EDGE OF A NEW FRONTIER —THE FRONTIER OF THE 1960s, A FRONTIER OF UNKNOWN OPPORTUNITIES AND PERILS, A FRONTIER OF UNFULFILLED HOPES AND THREATS. THE NEW FRONTIER OF WHICH I SPEAK IS NOT A SET OF PROMISES—IT IS A SET OF CHALLENGES."**
>
> John F. Kennedy, 1960

jostled for position in life. Before, if you wanted to be "posh" (middle-class or higher), you tried to speak BBC English, or "Received Pronunciation," but now, local and working-class accents were, if not celebrated, then regularly heard on TV, in plays, and on the radio.

The new decade brought a new desire to look and act differently, too. Young

people ceased to dress like their middle-aged parents and eagerly adopted new attitudes, new values, and new fashions, using a palette of ideas and appearances that both borrowed from and shaped popular music, cinema, fashion, magazines, and books.

Further changes were afoot in education. In 1960, the British government had woken up to the potential of the creative industry by commissioning and publishing the Coldstream Report on art and design education, leading, in 1963, to the new Diploma in Art and Design. By 1963, the Robbins Report had enabled working-class students (such as this author) to enter art colleges to study for the new Diploma, with fees and maintenance costs paid by the state.

The state funding of universities was seen as a necessary step to widen access and encourage more working-class students to apply: the number of UK universities doubled in the sixties, and the new "plateglass" universities (such as Essex, Lancaster, York, Warwick, UEA, Kent, and Sussex) were not only distinguished by their unique architecture, and by the courses they offered, but by the number of working-class students who went to them. Meanwhile, an expanding art-school system was feeding a developing creative scene, propelling fresh new talent into the growing fashion, art, design, music, TV, and movie businesses.

Musicians such as Keith Richards, Brian Eno, David Bowie, John Lennon, and Pete Townshend all came from an art-college background that encouraged imagination and independent thinking. As Brian Eno said in an interview with the *Guardian* in 2012, "When the recording studio suddenly really took off as a tool, it was the kids from art school who knew how to use it, not the kids from music school. . . . Music students were all stuck in the notion of music as performance, ephemeral. Whereas for an art student . . . music as painting? They knew how to do that."

Popular music was going through big changes by the time the Beatles and their manager, Brian Epstein, left Liverpool and arrived in London in the summer of 1963. Their debut studio album, *Please Please Me*, was released in 1963, shortly after the band signed with Dick James to form Northern Songs in Dick James's offices on the corner of "Tin Pan Alley"—formally known as Denmark Street.

For half a century, the street had been the traditional home of music

publishing, but was then in decline, along with the worlds of variety theater and music hall, as the new age of recording and broadcasting developed. Fifties songwriters such as Jimmy Kennedy (best known for "Red Sails in the Sunset" and "Teddy Bears' Picnic"), artists such as Johnnie Ray and Alma Cogan, and publishers such as Mills Music were going out of fashion. At this time, Elton John was a tea boy at Mills Music, which rejected Paul Simon's "Homeward Bound" and "The Sound of Silence" as being uncommercial.

Denmark Street was changing, recording studios and music shops replacing traditional music publishing. Teenagers were rehearsing at home, too, making their own new kind of music, honing their talents to help create what would become an industry of global importance. As Stuart

Nicholson writes in his book *Jazz-Rock: A History*, "By 1961 in Liverpool alone there were 273 garage bands playing some 300 clubs in the city. . . . By 1964, 40 percent of the population of the US was under twenty."

Teenagers would now enjoy an unprecedented level of affluence, and their enormous purchasing power made them a desirable target for the "cultural industries." The rise of rock 'n' roll brought a new kind of entertainer, songwriter, and recording artist who played new types of venues, supervised by a new breed of manager—and the new teenage audience loved what was on offer.

But the British broadcast media had failed to keep up with any of these new developments, or to cater to the new teenage thirst for rock 'n' roll. For several years in the late fifties and early sixties, the only outlet for pop music on radio

was *Saturday Club* (first broadcast as *Saturday Skiffle Club*), on which a mix of records by the likes of Cliff Richard, Humphrey Lyttelton, and Adam Faith could be heard. The Beatles would appear on the show ten times during 1963 and '64. On TV, the BBC's *Juke Box Jury* featured a guest panel that reviewed new releases, judging which was a "hit" and which a "miss," for twenty-five minutes per week . . . and that was it, until the BBC introduced the weekly *Top of the Pops*.

Ready Steady Go!, first broadcast on ITV in 1963 and initially hosted by Keith Fordyce, marked the beginning of a revolution in British rock-and-pop television. (It was shown in the States as *RSG USA!*) For a start, from 1964 on, it was hosted not by an older man but by a *teenager*, Cathy McGowan, who interviewed musicians from the leading

bands of the day in an open, natural way, using teenage slang. She soon became a celebrity in her own right, known as "Queen of the Mods" due to her dress style. At first, bands on *RSG* lip-synched to their records, but by 1964 some of the guests actually played live—and by 1965, the show had switched to all-live performances.

RSG was a huge success on TV, but the situation on radio remained dire—and radio remained important, as most British homes only had one TV, shared by the whole family. Pop coverage on BBC radio was limited to "Pick of the Pops"—itself only a slot in *Trad Tavern*, about jazz, until 1961—which ran through the Top 20 every Saturday evening. (It moved to Sunday evening in 1962, also becoming a separate program in its own right that year.) Teens could resort to Radio Luxembourg ("Lux"), but had to wait for the pirate stations to hear some real action.

The first "pirate" station to go on air, Radio Caroline—"Your all-day music station"—started broadcasting in March 1964, from off the east coast of England—just out of British territorial waters, beyond the reach of the British authorities (hence the "pirate" label). Radio Caroline North launched in July (enabling the station to reach all of Britain), and Radio London ("Big L") followed in December 1964. With its American-style jingles and slick DJs, Big L was as refreshing, and popular, as Radio Caroline.

ABOVE LEFT: The Beatles pose on a rooftop with toy instruments, 1964.

ABOVE: George Harrison kisses his new wife, the model Pattie Boyd, at a press conference held on January 22, 1966, to announce their marriage the previous day.

RIGHT: Radio Caroline, broadcasting from international waters off the east coast of England, summer 1964.

FAR RIGHT: Fans of Radio London mob the station's DJs at Liverpool Street station following its final broadcast on August 15, 1967.

By 1967, ten pirate stations were operating, reaching an audience of up to fifteen million people. The BBC was left standing, so far as the teen and rock/pop audience was concerned, and was (eventually) forced into opening its own rock and pop channel, Radio 1, in 1967. At the same time, the pirate stations were closed by an act of parliament. They'd played a major role in bringing pop music to the teens and rock 'n' roll fans of Britain at a critical time in the sixties.

SWINGIN' INTO LONDON

In moving to London in 1963—first to the Hotel President during the summer and then to a shared flat near Hyde Park—the Beatles arrived just when big changes were happening, or about to happen. A wind of change truly was in the air, even if it perhaps wasn't quite the kind of change envisaged by Macmillan or promised by Wilson (instead, it brought national scandals and a sense of decay in the political establishment, but also optimism about the educational and other reforms, and the breaking down of Britain's old class barriers).

London, and London life itself, was changing too. The pall of fifties London's smog, dirt, and general grayness was being swept aside by the saturated palette of psychedelic culture: the city was establishing itself as "Swinging London." The Beatles' circumstances were to change with the move as well.

> **IN ALL OUR PLANS FOR THE FUTURE, WE ARE REDEFINING AND WE ARE RESTATING OUR SOCIALISM IN TERMS OF THE SCIENTIFIC REVOLUTION. BUT THAT REVOLUTION CANNOT BECOME A REALITY UNLESS WE ARE PREPARED TO MAKE FAR-REACHING CHANGES IN ECONOMIC AND SOCIAL ATTITUDES."** Harold Wilson, 1963

They'd meet many new people in London—people who would have a profound impact on their lives and work over the ensuing years. A live BBC concert recording at the Royal Albert

Hall brought Paul McCartney together with Jane Asher, a beautiful seventeen-year-old actress who had achieved early fame as a child actress, and who would later appear in *Alfie* (1966), with Michael Caine, and Jerzy Skolimowski's *Deep End* (1970); their meeting would in turn bring McCartney into contact with the London counterculture through Barry Miles and his Indica Gallery and Bookshop, while McCartney was staying at the Asher family home.

The relatively small numbers of people involved in the counterculture and their proximity to each other was an important element in the development of the London underground scene. Around two or three hundred people would be actively involved in the early days of the counterculture, and they were all based within a dense cluster of central London postal addresses. Interactions often happened through chance meetings in local streets. Connections were made and friendships established all within a short journey by cycle or Mini Moke® (the small car of choice for those in the know) between people's apartments and key venues.

Each London area, or "village," was different—some were expensive, some run-down and cheap, though fast becoming gentrified. Some areas were considered the heart of fashion or were centers for alternative culture and artists' studios; others were the focus of social and political activity. These included the Docklands area near Tower Bridge in East London; Islington and Chalk Farm in North London; Notting Hill Gate, Westbourne Grove, and Chelsea in West and Southwest

ABOVE LEFT: Paul McCartney and his actress girlfriend Jane Asher attend the premiere of *Alfie* at the Plaza Theatre, London, March 25, 1966.

ABOVE: McCartney gets a light from Barry Miles at the opening of the Indica Gallery while Paul's friend Maggie McGivern looks on, spring 1966.

LEFT: An elegantly dressed woman drives her friend around the streets of Paris in a Mini Moke, spring 1966.

London; and Holborn and Soho in central London.

The move to London would bring the Beatles into contact with the salon culture of the underground and the homes and apartments of friends, which could offer safe spaces for marijuana-fueled conversations and LSD-shaped experiences. Michael Hollingshead arrived in London from the US in 1965 with half a gram of lysergic acid diethylamide (LSD), enough apparently for 5,000 acid trips. Hollingshead, a British researcher in psychedelic drugs invited to teach at Harvard University by Timothy Leary shortly after introducing Leary to LSD, reputedly "turned on" the whole London scene from his World Psychedelic Centre, located at his flat in Pont Street, Belgravia. This was at a time when LSD was legal in Britain; it was banned in the summer of 1966, and in California in October of the same year. Those reportedly turned on by Hollingshead include jazz musician Charles Mingus, Eric Clapton, Paul McCartney, Donovan, Keith Richards, Beat poet Allen Ginsberg, psychiatrist R. D. Laing, filmmaker Roman Polanski and his girlfriend Sharon Tate, and novelist William S. Burroughs.

It was considered good practice at the time to take LSD only in the company of others experienced in "tripping." Trips varied depending on personal mood and the general atmosphere. For some, LSD could create moments of intense concentration that would enhance listening experience and visual stimulus. On one occasion, I found myself wandering down Kensington Church Street in West London on a "psychotropic tour," having taken LSD with Michael English, partner, with Nigel Waymouth, of the influential design partnership Hapshash & the Coloured Coat, and the soon-to-be-famous Martin Sharp, artist and art editor of *OZ* magazine. We would stop for a long time to try to describe what we were looking at as we gazed on the chandeliers in a high-street lighting shop and later paused to admire the pattern of brick on the wall of a local building . . . and so it would go for a whole afternoon.

Peoples' apartments would provide a window into the interests of those active on the alternative scene, their passions collected on their bookshelves and in the objects, lifestyles, and record collections found in their living spaces.

Everybody Must Get Stoned

ON AUGUST 28, 1964, a meeting of minds took place at the Delmonico Hotel in New York that would forever change the course of popular music. It was here that Bob Dylan and the Beatles were first introduced to one another by a mutual friend, the journalist Al Aronowitz—and that Dylan introduced the Beatles to marijuana.

Though it was not quite the first time the band had encountered the drug, Harrison later recalling that he had been encouraged to smoke it by "an older drummer with another group in Liverpool," it was the first time they became fully aware of the mind-bending creative possibilities it would open up. For his part, Dylan had assumed the band were already *au fait*, having misheard the chorus of "I Want to Hold Your Hand" as "I get high, I get high, I get high." After a sheepish Lennon revealed that the line was actually "I can't hide," Dylan and Aronowitz started rolling joints, and the Beatles and their cohorts began to relax and float upstream.

The impact of the drug was profound. McCartney would later describe how he felt that he was "thinking for the first time"; so convinced was he that a major creative breakthrough might occur at any moment, he had roadie Mal Evans

follow him around the hotel with a notepad, ready to write down anything Paul said. Manager Brian Epstein, meanwhile, was "so high I'm on the ceiling." And it didn't stop there. Before long, as Ringo later put it, the band would be "smoking pot for breakfast."

Pot and Dylan would prove to be perhaps the two biggest influences on the Beatles' work in the mid-sixties. The band had first heard his *Freewheelin'* album, containing such hard-hitting, topical tracks as "Blowin' in the Wind" and "Masters of War," earlier in 1964, and would listen to it continuously while on tour that spring. For Lennon in particular, it served as an artistic wake-up call. The Beatles' early hits, though often deceptively complex, had been intended primarily for a teenybopper audience more interested in dancing than poetry, and for John that would no longer be enough. As far as he was concerned, those songs lacked

emotional depth; listening to Dylan, on record and in person, he was struck by the need to express himself and his feelings rather than merely project himself objectively into a song's narrative. The impact of that realization is clear in the emotional and stylistic depth of songs such as "You've Got to Hide Your Love Away" (from *Help!*) and "Norwegian Wood" (from *Rubber Soul*).

McCartney, too, became a more nuanced and explorative writer. By the time of songs such as "She's Leaving Home," written for *Sgt. Pepper*, the pair had developed full and individual songwriting voices. That song offered a poignant reimaging of a newspaper story of a young runaway, with Paul's verses depicting the parents' discovery that their daughter has left and Lennon's chorus unpicking their conflicting emotions as they reconcile her disappearance with the sacrifices they made during her childhood, all

RIGHT: Bob Dylan's breakthrough second album, *The Freewheelin' Bob Dylan*, released by Columbia in 1963.

FAR RIGHT: Dylan looks out into space from the Mayfair Hotel, London, May 3, 1966.

delivered over a beautifully realized, sorrowful melody.

While that meeting at the Delmonico Hotel is largely thought of, rightly, as having had a huge impact on the Beatles' music, the influence was not entirely one way. Dylan, who would cause great consternation in the folk world in 1965 by "going electric," was clearly invigorated by the fresh exuberance of the Beatles' approach and sound. Mid-sixties songs such as "It Ain't Me, Babe" and "4th Time Around," the latter a playful response to

> **I WROTE SONGS FOR THE MEAT MARKET, AND I DIDN'T CONSIDER THEM, THE LYRICS OR ANYTHING, TO HAVE ANY DEPTH AT ALL. IT WAS DYLAN WHO HELPED ME REALIZE THAT."** John Lennon, 1971

the marked Dylan feel of "Norwegian Wood," bear out that influence.

"Oh I get it," Dylan reportedly remarked to McCartney on hearing *Sgt. Pepper* for the first time. "You don't want to be cute anymore." He would remain an admirer of the band, and became particularly close to Harrison, with

whom he worked on several occasions during the seventies, eighties, and nineties. In 2007, looking out across the musical landscape, he described McCartney as "about the only one that I am in awe of," while his 2012 album *Tempest* includes a fourteen-minute tribute to Lennon, "Roll on, John."

THE MOOD

27

These provided new insights for the Beatles as their art matured toward the creation of their 1965 album *Rubber Soul*, an artistic work made in a new way in a single period of writing and continuous studio recording, over the course of a month. That album would articulate a wider mix of influences, from soul to folk to world music, introducing new exotic sounds such as the sitar playing of George Harrison . . . all hinting at things to come.

Two of the most influential figures in the development of the underground were John "Hoppy" Hopkins and the aforementioned Barry Miles. Miles first met Hoppy in late 1959 when living as an art student in Cheltenham in the west of England. Miles, who often hitchhiked to London, was offered a room to stay in Hoppy's flat on Westbourne Terrace, a gesture much

appreciated as Miles began his love affair with bohemian life and a long, fruitful relationship with the capital city.

Hoppy had graduated from Cambridge University at the age of twenty with a degree in physics and mathematics and worked for the Atomic Energy Research Establishment until a trip to the Soviet Union, and the gift of a camera, changed his life. The trip to Russia led to a security interview in Whitehall (the seat of the British government) and a *Daily Mirror* headline announcing that the Soviets had been propositioning an English nuclear physicist.

The camera offered Hoppy the opportunity to get out of nuclear physics in 1960 and start a career as a London photojournalist, working for papers such as *Melody Maker* and *Peace News*. Because of his young age and lack of

TOP LEFT: John "Hoppy" Hopkins at home circa. early 1960.

TOP: Merry Prankster Ken Kesey and his wife, Faye, attend a happening in San Francisco, 1966.

ABOVE: "All your dreams are true at Indica," according to this 1967 *International Times* ad for the bookshop at its new premises on Southampton Row.

> **WHAT KEEPS US FROM BEING MONSTERS ARE EMERSON AND THOREAU AND THE BEATLES AND BOB DYLAN— GREAT ARTISTS WHO TEACH US TO LOVE AND HOLD OFF ON THE HURT."** Ken Kesey, 1994

cash, Miles could not accompany Hoppy on his trip to the USSR, though access to Hoppy's flat meant he could spend more time in London visiting his favorite areas, like Soho, with its bookshops and boho culture, typified by venues such as the New Left stronghold the Partisan Coffee House. A permanent move in 1963 offered Miles the chance to work at the Better Books store on Charing Cross Road.

Meanwhile, by the end of 1964, Hoppy had moved into a large five-bedroom flat in an Edwardian block in Notting Hill Gate, West London, the hotbed of London's counterculture scene. His new home became an important hub and center of activity, functioning on various occasions as a design and publishing center; a crash-pad for international travelers on their way to the Far East via the "hippie trail"; an agitprop meeting space; an information center for fellow countercultural visitors from the US and Europe; and as a party and event space, too. A steady stream of people, information, material, and drugs flowed into London from various scenes abroad and filtered through portals such as Hoppy's flat and, later, the Indica Bookshop, along with other leading underground distribution centers such

as Compendium Books in Camden High Street, North London; Housmans Bookshop in Caledonian Road; and the Students' Union at the London School of Economics, in Houghton Street.

Through the grapevine came news of an event that became known as the "Red Dog Experience" in Virginia City, Nevada, an all-night psychedelic experience at the Red Dog Saloon, a refurbished Wild West bar where people wore turn-of-the-century gear, combining a traditional folk look with a developing psychedelic-rock sound and aesthetic. The event was first held privately in 1963, before being opened to the public in the summer of 1965. There was no clear distinction between performers and the proto-hippie audience at the "happening," which featured a basic light show organized by Bill Ham (later to manage ZZ Top) and presented then-unknown musical acts such as San Francisco band Big Brother & the Holding Company, and the Charlatans.

In the meantime, Ken Kesey, author of *One Flew Over the Cuckoo's Nest* (1962), began hosting happenings with friends after his move to La Honda, California, in 1963. In June 1964, he embarked on his "Further" tour across the US,

traveling from San Francisco to New York in an old Harvester school bus (with "Further" listed on the destination panel at the front) with the Merry Pranksters, a group that included Neal Cassady, who had appeared, as Dean Moriarty, in Jack Kerouac's 1957 book *On the Road*. Acid-test happenings were held along the way. Kesey decided to go public with his own parties in November 1965, advertising an "acid test" in a private home, with the Merry Pranksters providing light shows and music provided by Kesey's own Psychedelic Symphonette. More shows followed in various venues, finally arriving at San Francisco's Fillmore Auditorium on January 8, 1966, when 2,400 blissed-out attendees listened to the Grateful Dead while banks of audiovisual equipment created a backdrop of light and sound.

The opening of the Psychedelic Shop in the Haight-Ashbury district of San Francisco in January 1966 reflected a cultural shift in the city, as a huge influx of young kids came looking for an alternative universe to that on offer in the parental home. This concentration of young hippies looking to create a social experiment would produce practical problems and a backlash from the local authorities.

Around this time, the Diggers, a local anarchist community, would set up shelters for new arrivals in Haight-Ashbury, providing twenty-four-hour help and a permanent free lawyer on Haight Street as part of a legal-aid program. In their statement of ideology the Diggers stated, "Everything we do is free because we are failures. We've got nothing, so we've got nothing to lose."

Over on the East Coast, meanwhile, Andy Warhol staged his first "Exploding Plastic Inevitable" at a dinner for the New York Society for Clinical Psychiatry on January 13, 1966. The event, titled "Up-Tight," included performances by the Velvet Underground & Nico, with Gerard Malanga and Edie Sedgwick appearing as dancers and filmmaker Barbara Rubin as a performance artist. Further shows were held at the Dom, the East Village's hippest nightspot on St. Mark's Place, and in various other cities.

Counterculture news from the US would arrive in London courtesy of the underground free press, with updates on current activities on both American coasts. These activities would be commented on and reported on by a growing alternative press, including: the *Los Angeles Free Press*, established in May 1964 by Art Kunkin and cited as the first underground newspaper; the influential *Berkeley Barb*, a very political, anti–Vietnam War paper founded in August 1965 by Max Scherr; and the New York–based *East Village Other*, co-founded in October 1965 by Walter Bowart and Ishmael Reed, a bi-weekly that started out using Dada type montages and developed into a full-blown colorful psychedelic layout featuring comic strips by Robert Crumb and Art Spiegelman.

GETTING BETTER

Back in Britain, a key moment in terms of increasing the visibility of the London counterculture occurred in May 1965, when the poet Allen Ginsberg—best known for "Howl"—came to London and met Miles at Better Books. Miles, who was managing the paperback section at the time, offered the homeless Ginsberg a room at his Hanson Street flat. In return, Ginsberg offered a free reading at Better Books, which he gave to a packed-out room. Half of those in the audience were American—including Andy Warhol and Edie Sedgwick.

Better Books, influenced by San Francisco's City Lights Bookstore, was the center of English beat culture.

ABOVE: The Velvet Underground & Nico perform at one of Andy Warhol's "Exploding Plastic Inevitable" events, the Dom, New York City, April 1, 1966.

It offered a template for an emerging counterculture as a multidisciplinary arts-center experience with a gallery and cinema; a stage for readings, talks, and performance; and a creative atmosphere that welcomed new art forms such as assemblage, performance art, and radical poetry. According to Hoppy Hopkins, "There were some really great happenings at Better Books, a room full of smoke and people sitting around and falling over each other, and

it was terribly erotic, something you weren't expecting at all."

After a fire in late 1964, the basement was given over to happenings. The inaugural event was staged by poet, artist, and musician Jeff Nuttall and conceptual artist John Latham; by 1965, the bookstore was the cradle of British underground film, itself initiated by Nuttall. That year, the sound, visual, and performance poet Bob Cobbing, who had been running film societies in

Within and Without

FOR THE FOUR BEATLES and so many others, the mid-sixties were a time of great exploration—of different ideas, cultures, belief systems, and more. And for George Harrison in particular, that exploration would yield profound changes in both his life and his musical approach.

Harrison's interest in Eastern philosophy and music began to crystalize in 1965. First, during the filming of *Help!* in the Bahamas at the beginning of the year, he and the other Beatles met Swami Vishnu Devananda, the founder of Sivananda Yoga, who presented each of them with a copy of his 1959 work *The Complete Illustrated Book of Yoga*. Then, during the summer, Harrison was introduced by David Crosby of the Byrds to the sound of the sitar and the work of its foremost exponent, Ravi Shankar.

Before long, he would be playing the instrument himself on the distinctive opening to "Norwegian Wood," the second track on *Rubber Soul*, released at the very end of 1965. The song itself is widely credited with introducing Indian music to a Western pop audience, but for Harrison, this was only the beginning of what would prove to be a lifelong journey.

Harrison's search for more nuanced spiritual ideas followed a nineteenth-century tendency to seek answers in Eastern ideas and philosophy, offering a way of being that appealed to bohemian society and avant-garde culture in the West. Interest in the East and the pursuit of individual spiritual journeys was prevalent across sixties culture, featured in the works of the poet Allen Ginsberg, musicians Pete Townshend and Donovan, the painter Robert Indiana, and the philosopher and writer Alan Watts, who wrote the hugely influential *The Way of Zen* (1957). Watts gave the first lecture at the California-based Esalen Institute, founded in 1963, which itself became the nexus of counterculture thinking in the sixties, and would be central to the later development of New Age thinking.

When the Beatles took a break from performing and recording in the summer of 1966, George and his new wife, Pattie, embarked upon a six-week trip to India, where Harrison would study the sitar under Shankar and meet with the Maharishi Mahesh Yogi, whose teachings would have a profound impact on all four Beatles over the next few years. At George's urging, they would all study Transcendental Meditation under the Maharishi following the completion of work on *Sgt. Pepper*.

Hindu philosophy emphasizes the importance of the teacher and his relationship with the aspirant—a relationship devised as a way of managing ego in the journey to self-definition. Hindu teaching highlights the importance of *dharma* and *karma*. Dharma is the law of being, where moral law combines with discipline to provide an ethical glue in daily life; karma provides the concept of reincarnation that determines the state of an individual in the next existence. Harrison firmly believed that "life on

> **I AM NOT REALLY 'BEATLE GEORGE.' 'BEATLE GEORGE' IS LIKE A SUIT OR SHIRT THAT I ONCE WORE ON OCCASION AND UNTIL THE END OF MY LIFE PEOPLE MAY SEE THAT SHIRT AND MISTAKE IT FOR ME."** George Harrison, 1995

Earth is but a fleeting illusion edged between lives past and future beyond physical mortal reality." Speaking on reincarnation in 1968, he said, "You go on being reincarnated until you reach the actual Truth."

Hindu practice also offers techniques such as meditation to aid a condition of unity between mind and body, as a way of accessing the metaphysical through the mundane physical world, linking the microcosm with the macrocosm, as a means to achieving happiness and bliss in daily life.

Though Harrison was encouraged by the Maharishi to stop taking LSD, the sensory experience of psychotropic drugs was certainly enhanced by listening to the "groove" of Indian classical music, which itself would prove a major influence on sonic developments in psychedelic music. In fact, though, listening to the meditative sounds of a classical *raga* (or *raag*) can create a natural "high" without the aid of artificial stimulants. The raga, which literally means color/hue and beauty/melody, is defined more by the way notes are

approached and rendered in musical phrases to convey mood, rather than the notes themselves. Sliding notes that bend and float are stretched into long, drone-like passages of sound. These passages ascend and descend (an essential raga feature) with pace and rhythm—divided into slow, medium, and fast—to create a sound as soulful and expressive as blues slide guitar.

Add to raga the extemporizing sound of the voice, and you create a totally immersive experience. Performances can last for many hours, from dusk till dawn in some cases, as part of a musical form that is categorized and shaped by the time of the day or night in which it is played. The performer improvises and composes on the spot, making music that is not written down but simply remembered, an action described as "painting on a canvas of silence," creating emotional and psychological responses. Each raga has its own principal mood, be it love, humor, pathos, anger, heroism, terror, disgust, or wonder. Raga, which is several thousand years old, is difficult to sustain in an increasingly noisy and busy world.

Harrison's ever-growing passion for Indian culture is clear in songs such as *Sgt. Pepper*'s seventh track, "Within You Without You," a composition in the Indian classical style inspired by his six-week stay in India with Ravi Shankar in 1966, and performed with members of the Asian Music Circle rather than with the other Beatles.

These interests are further reflected in the appearance of yogis such as Paramahansa Yogananda, an influential teacher, and Sri Yukteswar Giri, author of *The Holy Science*, among the crowd depicted on the album cover.

North London, began showing movies at Better Books under the name "Cinema 65," concentrating on avant-garde works such as Jack Smith's *Flaming Creatures* (1963) and Kenneth Anger's *Scorpio Rising* (1964), as well as offering open screenings.

The bookstore eventually became a base for the London Film-Makers' Co-operative, which was formed in October 1966 and included Stephen Dwoskin, who had flown over from New York to teach design at the London College of Printing. Dwoskin's movies include *Asleep* (1961) and *Chinese Checkers* (1964–1965). Other members included: Cobbing; the artist and poet Jeff Keen, who created his *Marvo Movie* in 1967; and producer and activist Simon Hartog. Based on a model inspired by the New York and other international film co-ops, the LFMC sought to provide exhibition and distribution facilities, and also published a journal, *Cinim*. (It would relocate to Jim Haynes's Drury Lane Arts Lab after Better Books closed in October 1967.)

It was at Miles's Hanson Street flat that a plan began to form to create a large poetry event after the experience of the packed Ginsberg readings at

Better Books. The timing was good, as a number of poets happened to be nearby in London and Paris. A small group of people, including filmmaker Barbara Rubin, Barry and Sue Miles, Alex Trocchi, Michael Horowitz, and Hoppy Hopkins came together and organized the "International Poetry Incarnation," which took place at London's Royal Albert Hall on June 11, 1965. The day-long event saw the first large-scale coming together of the nascent London counterculture, a gathering of 8,000 people waving flowers collected unsold from Covent Garden Flower Market and handed out by Kate Heliczer (an émigré from the Andy Warhol factory in New York) and friends, their faces painted in psychedelic patterns. Attendees would listen to readings by international poets in an atmosphere hung heavy with the aroma of blossoms and pot. It was a day of some chaos (and mixed performances), with revelers blissed-out in balcony boxes and groups picnicking amongst the stalls. The audience (which included Indira Gandhi, who would become prime minister of India the following year) became the beating heart of the happening, creating the atmosphere

and "far-out" listening mood for the poets' performances. Readings of the day included, among others, Allen Ginsberg; fellow Beat poet Gregory Corso; progressive poet and key counterculture figure Michael Horowitz; Simon Vinkenoog, a member of the Dutch cultural-provocateur movement Provo; Lawrence Ferlinghetti, the co-founder of City Lights Bookshop in San Francisco; English novelist and playwright Adrian Mitchell, who gave a powerful reading of "To Whom It May Concern (Tell Me Lies About Vietnam)"; Austrian writer and poet Ernst Jandl, who performed ten minutes of sneezing in homage to the German artist Kurt Schwitters; and American novelist William S. Burroughs, who didn't read but played a tape over the Albert Hall's PA system.

Miles was well read and informed on contemporary American literature, Beat culture, and the English and European avant-garde, as well as London's bohemian life. Better Books offered a platform for increased links to alternative cultures in the US and promotion of experimental events through the store. Both Hoppy and Miles possessed great energy, excellent networking skills, engaging and

generous personalities, and a love of communicating in print through words and pictures. They established Lovebooks Limited after the 1965 Albert Hall reading, first publishing a spoken-word recording of poetry and *Darazt*, an anthology of poems and Hoppy photography in the form of a little magazine. This was followed by *Long Hair Times*, an eighty-page literary

magazine. Toward the end of 1966, they would establish the *International Times*, which soon became the house paper of the British counterculture.

After the sale of Better Books to the rather more traditional booksellers Hatchards, Miles set out to open his own bookshop. John Dunbar, who was interested in opening a gallery, teamed up with Miles and brought in his friend,

Peter Asher, to form the company Miles, Asher, and Dunbar Limited (MAD). Dunbar, an artist, collector, and gallerist who had recently married the singer Marianne Faithfull (with Asher as best man), found suitable premises at 6 Mason's Yard in the St. James's district of London, where the Indica Bookshop and Gallery opened in September 1965. As well as being the brother of Jane Asher,

OPPOSITE: Allen Ginsberg gives a reading in Kensington in advance of the "International Poetry Incarnation" at the Royal Albert Hall, May 1966.

ABOVE: British artist John Dunbar (*left*) and writer/bookseller Barry Miles (*right*) surrounded by painting and decorating materials during internal construction of the Indica Bookshop and Gallery, London, late 1965.

Peter was one half of the successful Peter & Gordon singing duo, famous for their 1964 hit "A World Without Love," penned by Paul McCartney.

Peter had arranged for Miles to use the basement of his parents' house on Wimpole Street as a stockroom while Indica was being refurbished for the opening. Paul McCartney, now living with Jane and her parents, would wander down to the basement and select the occasional book, leaving an IOU as payment. Books he selected included *Peace Eye Poems* by Ed Sanders and *Gandhi on Non-violence*.

As their friendship grew, Miles would introduce McCartney to the works of Burroughs and Ginsberg and talk with him about Buddhism, drugs, and "pataphysics," a term coined by French writer Alfred Jarry to describe, among other things, a science of imaginary solutions (such as speculative string theory). McCartney, for his part, offered a helping hand in preparing Indica for the opening by lending his car for pickups and drop-offs, doing occasional bits of DIY during renovation of the premises, helping to draw flyers announcing the forthcoming opening, and hand-drawing and producing 1,000 sheets of wrapping paper.

Art dealer Robert Fraser, a friend of John Dunbar, was a neighbor of Indica. His apartment was just above the Scotch of St. James club in Mason's Yard, Westminster. Fraser was a member of the aristocratic Chelsea set whose home salon was frequented by old-money aristocrats, pop stars, and other key figures of the time. His Dover Street gallery exhibited the rising stars of

sixties art, including Andy Warhol, Bridget Riley, and David Hockney. At one time, Fraser removed the gallery window to exhibit a Cobra sports car owned by Tara Browne, the Guinness heir, hand-painted by the design team Binder Edwards & Vaughan. Browne was killed in a motor accident in December 1966—an event referenced by John Lennon, his friend, in the Beatles' song "A Day in the Life." It was through Robert Fraser's friendship with Dunbar that John Lennon connected with the developing counterculture . . . which in turn led to Lennon's first meeting with Yoko Ono at her Indica show, "Unfinished Paintings and Objects," in November 1966.

TAKE A TRIP

The London club scene provided venues for the developing psychedelic scene as well as a kick-start for the career of practically every key rock figure of the sixties, not to mention prime meeting places for an emerging hippie and Swinging London scene. Alternative clubs that catered to the growing underground audience included UFO, the first psychedelic club in Britain, on Tottenham Court Road, and Middle Earth, in Covent Garden, hosted by DJ and promoter Jeff Dexter, which featured most of the big-name performers at the time.

Other clubs on the Swinging London scene included the Scotch of St. James on Mason's Yard, a prominent nightclub, music venue, and meeting place for rock musicians, and the place where Jimi Hendrix played his first UK solo gig in September 1966. The Bag O' Nails on Kingly Street, Soho, was a favorite venue of Paul McCartney, and was where he met his future wife Linda Eastman, a few weeks after completing work on *Sgt. Pepper*. The Speakeasy Club on Margaret Street was a meeting place for the record industry, where emerging bands played, hoping to be spotted. The Marquee Club, at 90 Wardour Street, opened in 1958 with jazz and skiffle acts and became another key venue. The 100 Club on Oxford Street, a legendary venue, opened its doors in 1942.

OPPOSITE, FAR LEFT: BEV design partners Dudley Edwards (*left*) and Doug Binder with the Cobra sports car they hand-painted for Tara Browne.

OPPOSITE, LEFT: Yoko Ono poses beside her famous *Apple*, Indica Gallery, November 14, 1966.

ABOVE: An *International Times* ad for Ono's debut Indica Gallery show.

RIGHT: Silkscreen poster designed by Mike McInnerney for a UFO club "Dusk to Dawn" event featuring Arthur Brown, Alexis Korner, Tomorrow, and the Bonzo Dog Doo-Dah Band, July 14 and 21, 1967.

LEFT: British model Twiggy, the *Daily Mirror*'s "Face of 1966," talks to friends at Blaise's, London, spring 1967.

The Flamingo R&B and Jazz Club in Soho played an important role in the development of jazz and British rhythm and blues during the sixties; the Troubadour coffee house on Old Brompton Road, West London, provided a primary venue for the British folk revival in its basement, as did Bunjies in Litchfield Street, one of the original folk cafes, which opened in 1954. (Tom Paxton, John Renbourn, Bert Jansch, Bob Dylan, Al Stewart, and Paul Simon all performed here, in the 400-year-old wine cellar, early in their careers.)

Shops and boutiques began to cater to the new tastes and attitudes of a growing hippie culture. Outlets such as Hung on You and Granny Takes a Trip were not only at the vanguard of fashion but also provided meeting places and distribution centers for the latest news from the underground, in much the same way as did bookshops like Indica and Compendium. In addition, galleries such as the Environmental Art Gallery, run by Keith Albarn at 26 Kingly Street; the Signals Gallery, on Wigmore Street; and the Arts Lab, on Drury Lane, would provide appropriate arguments, ideas, and visual statements in support of contemporary attitudes.

One particular club would play an important part in the developing counterculture, providing the first venue for the early psychedelic underground scene. Spontaneous Underground

RIGHT: A fashionably dressed girl looks out onto Cale Street, London, from the hip boutique Hung on You, July 1966.

FAR RIGHT: Music fans— including one holding a copy of the Rolling Stones' *Aftermath*— relaxing at Hung on You.

> " **THE SPONTANEOUS UNDERGROUND . . . BECAME THE VILLAGE PUMP OF THE UNDERGROUND, WITH SOMETHING OF THE PARTY ATMOSPHERE OF THE ALBERT HALL READING. THERE WAS NO ALCOHOL BUT PLENTY OF POT AND ACID."** Barry Miles, 2002

opened in January 1966 as a Sunday-afternoon happening in the hired space of the Marquee Club. It was started by an American, Steve Stollman, whose brother ran the New York label ESP, America's foremost avant-garde record label, with the likes of Sun Ra, Albert Ayler, and Ornette Coleman on its roster.

According to a report in the *Sunday Times*, "The Spontaneous Underground was a happening where the invited are the entertainment . . . who will be there? Poets, painters, pop singers, clowns, jazz musicians, politicians, sculptors . . . this is underground culture, which offers everyone the opportunity to do or say anything without conforming to restrictions."

AMM, a free-form group of avant-garde experimentalists who performed in white lab coats, thus implying a scientific method to their music-making, played at Spontaneous Underground with Pink Floyd in June 1966. The group comprised Cornelius Cardew on piano, Lou Gare on tenor saxophone, Eddie Prévost on drums, Keith Rowe on electric guitar, and Lawrence Sheaff on cello (and also included violin,

xylophone, accordion, clarinet, and transistor radio in their repertoire of instruments). Cardew, who was Professor of Composition at the Royal College of Music, held weekly sound workshops with AMM in the basement of the college where, according to Miles, the audience would sit on the floor and the music could last for hours.

Miles and his wife Sue took Paul McCartney to one of Cardew's workshops in early 1966, to hear John Cage's theories of random sounds put into practice. In his book *In the Sixties*, Miles writes, "At this concert, the closest Cardew got to playing the piano was to tap its leg with a small piece of wood. Paul joined in by running a penny along the coils of the old-fashioned steam radiator." Miles also describes a further experimental music encounter

with Paul McCartney when they both attended a lecture at the Italian Institute in Belgravia by Luciano Berio, whose experimental work included nothing but speeded-up, heavily edited tapes of voices.

NEW TIMES

Pop and Op Art were also at the center of attention in London in the lead-up to the Summer of Love and launch of *Sgt. Pepper* in June 1967. Pop Art sampled popular culture for its subject matter, while Op Art examined the phenomena of optics and perception, creating work that confused and excited the eye. Op artists were also drawn to the idea of virtual movement through Kinetic Art.

Pop Art offered cultural currency in both the US, its spiritual home, and Britain, at the time. American Pop might better be described as art that sampled mass communication and shopping culture. The roots of British Pop, meanwhile, contained a domestic narrative bound in the popular culture of the working class, some of which is represented in the paintings of Peter Blake—work that adopted the culture of music hall entertainment, artists such as George Formby and Arthur English, the rise of celebrity culture, rock music, the cinema, the fairground, and the circus. His work celebrated English folk culture as well as emblematic forms such as targets, chevrons, and flags. These themes would influence London-based bands such as the Who, the Small Faces, and the Kinks—and the Beatles—as well as a developing fashion and media scene.

The growing interest in popular culture also contained elements of nostalgia that embraced Victorian art and design, Edwardian children's book

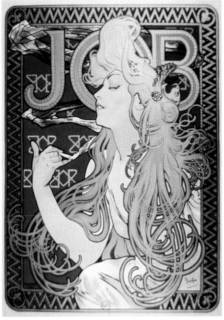

illustrators, vintage style clothing, and Art Nouveau, an end-of-era nineteenth-century art movement whose most influential exponents include Aubrey Beardsley and Alphonse Mucha. The Victoria and Albert Museum held a highly influential exhibition of Beardsley's work from May to September 1966. The sinuous organic forms expressed in the work of artists like Beardsley informed and shaped psychedelic graphic language for artists such as Michael English and Nigel Waymouth—and myself—and found expression in counterculture posters, newspapers, and magazines such as the *International Times* and *OZ*.

There was also another more oblique influence on psychedelic expression at that time. It took its palette of colors from the bright, playful, fully saturated hues of toys and children's illustrated books and its forms from the stylized world of cartoon drawing. Some would argue that the use of the rounded forms of Art Nouveau and the softer, non-threatening shapes and rainbow-colored elements of children's books were created to cope with the heightened sense of anxiety that can sometimes accompany the use of psychotropic drugs.

Two artists who best represent these aesthetics are the German graphic designer Heinz Edelmann, creator of the Beatles animated film *Yellow Submarine*, and the Australian artist and cartoonist Martin Sharp, newly arrived in London from Australia after an overland trek through Asia, via Kathmandu, with author Richard Neville. (They, along with fellow Australian Jim Anderson, would soon set up the London version of their Australian counterculture magazine *OZ*, with the first issue, published in February 1967, providing a full-color psychedelic commentary on the London scene.)

Op Art, an international movement that included Venezuelan artist Jesús Rafael Soto and Argentinian artist Julio LeParc, provided something to stare at while meditating on altered states of mind and the psychology of looking—the perfect form of contemplation for a counterculture exploring extreme experiences through psychotropic drugs. The immersive nature of the psychedelic experience, with the sonic and visual distortions of its music and hypnotic light shows, would echo the sensory nature of Op artists' work, much

The Million Volt Light and Sound Rave

The Roundhouse, London NW1
January 28 and February 8, 1967
By Dudley Edwards

IN THE EARLY SIXTIES, I formed a design partnership with Doug Binder and David Vaughan, who acted as agent/manager for the team. As Binder, Edwards & Vaughan (BEV), we established a reputation for high-quality painted psychedelic objects as part of the developing counterculture scene.

BEV was considered to be the Omega Workshop of its day—a reference to the pioneering studio founded in 1913 by members of the Bloomsbury Group, which rejected traditional distinctions between fine arts and decorative arts. BEV's interests also encompassed performance in the form of light shows for the psychedelic music scene.

Toward the end of 1966, we decided to hire the Roundhouse and produce the first concert of electronic music in England. We commissioned avant-garde electronic music from Unit Delta Plus, a groundbreaking freelance offshoot of the BBC's Radiophonic Workshop comprising Delia Derbyshire, Brian Hodgson, and Peter Zinovieff. I was also aware that Paul McCartney had been studying the music of Karlheinz Stockhausen at the time, and approached him with a request to participate in the concert. Paul agreed and was introduced to

Zinovieff at his studio in Putney, a concrete bunker at the bottom of his garden by the Thames with walls and ceiling constructed entirely of speakers. I was selected as a guinea pig for what proved to be one of the most amazing experiences of my life. Peter stood me in the center of the room and then switched on a tape of one of his compositions. The music was played at such intense decibel frequencies that many parts of my anatomy (including internal organs) began to perform an involuntary dance which could only be described as ecstatic twitching.

On the opening night of the Million Volt Light and Sound Rave, the BEV light show had to be seen to be believed. The whole interior of the dome was lined with a screen on which we projected moving images and fluid abstract shapes, often synchronized with the music. We had brought over Ray Anderson from the Fillmore

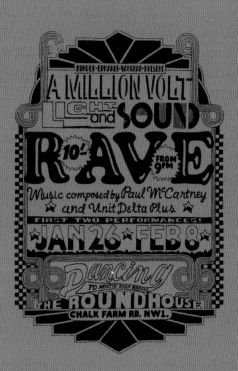

ABOVE: Bob Gill's poster for the Million Volt Light and Sound Rave.

> " WHEN THEY HAD FINISHED, GEORGE MARTIN SAID TO ME, 'THIS IS RIDICULOUS, WE'VE GOT TO GET OUR TEETH INTO SOMETHING MORE CONSTRUCTIVE.'" Geoff Emerick on "Carnival of Light"

concert hall in San Francisco to help with the lights during the two-night event. For the most part, the happening was received rapturously, the only exceptions being incidents of epilepsy and nausea.

Paul McCartney's electronic experiment, titled "Carnival of Light," lasted approximately fifteen minutes and is described by Beatles expert Mark Lewisohn as featuring "distorted, hypnotic drum and organ sounds, a distorted lead guitar, the sound of a church organ, various effects (water gargling was one) and, perhaps most

intimidating of all, John Lennon and McCartney screaming dementedly and bawling aloud random phrases like 'Are you all right?' and 'Barcelona!'" Other descriptions refer to a basic bed track of an organ playing bass notes and drums recorded at a fast speed that, when played back at a regular speed, sound deeper in pitch and slower in tempo. There was also a huge amount of reverb used on the instruments and on Lennon's and McCartney's vocals. The track concludes with McCartney asking the studio engineer, in an echo-soaked voice, "Can we hear it back now?"

Unfortunately, as Paul McCartney's electronic tape played we were unaware that stuck on the end of the recording was the first rendition of Paul singing his George Formby–inspired composition "Fixing a Hole," and nobody had the foresight to stop the tape. As it played, the audience was given the rare chance to hear, along with a miffed Paul McCartney, a song in development for the forthcoming *Sgt. Pepper* album. Luckily there were no bootleggers present.

Bob Harris later declared on his BBC radio show that this was one of the most memorable moments he experienced in the sixties. In a review titled "My Lost Psychedelic Week-End," written for the London *Evening Standard*, journalist Anne Sharpley recalled how "random music twisted inside our heads, well above the dangerous level. Two shadowy figures danced across a picture of the pope. Suzy Creamcheese 'freaked out.' The random music was made by using everything from a bicycle bell to a partly tuned transistor set. A deafening power of sound, a whole earful of lost enormous noises were released around us for two whole nights. Colored lights flooded the space and flashed around an international audience freaking out and finding it impossible to be still." When all the "noise" had subsided, Ray Anderson caught a plane back to the States; as we waved goodbye we were completely unaware that he was departing with a bag containing not only his fee but the tape of Paul's recording. To this day it remains the most sought-after piece of Beatles memorabilia.

as the perceptual illusions created in the paintings of Bridget Riley influenced the stark graphic patterns of hip sixties fashion styles.

The developing counterculture found inspiration in aspects of performance, happenings, and propaganda associated with the Situationist and Fluxus movements. The Situationist Group, formed in 1957, was a movement rooted in both politics and art that reached its peak in the social revolution of the French general strike in May 1968. One of the group's primary activities was visual propaganda through events and slogans in the form of graffiti and posters. Situationists questioned the way society commodified everything into something that can be bought and sold—for example, an image of Che Guevara, the Argentine Marxist revolutionary leader and a major figure in the Cuban Revolution, printed onto a T-shirt and sold at fashion stores. It was a movement that would herald the rise of conceptual art in the seventies; a deliberate anti-object, de-materialized form of art that was meant to be read rather than bought and sold or hung in galleries. Situationists sampled capitalist culture in order to subvert it and create environments favorable

to the fulfillment of human desires unmediated by capitalism. Meanwhile, Fluxus was an international and intermedia movement of artists, poets, composers, and designers noted for their experimental syntheses of different artistic media and disciplines, bringing together activities as diverse as art, poetry, economics, and chemistry. John Cage was an influence and Yoko Ono an exponent.

The Drury Lane Arts Lab, founded in 1967 by Jim Haynes, could be described as a Fluxus-type counterculture project, a new kind of arts center that inspired similar centers in the UK and continental Europe. Haynes was another important figure in the London underground scene, as well as a member of the *International Times* board. The Arts Lab was a space that offered something new in multidisciplinary experience, including gallery shows, poetry readings, a conference space, a cinema, a theater, music, and a wide range of alternative performance, as well as a hip cafe run by Sue Miles, a pivotal figure in the alternative scene in her own right.

On March 8, 1966, the London Free School held its first public meeting at St. Peter's Church Hall on Notting Hill Gate.

The school was an idea first discussed by Rhaune Laslett, a community activist, and Hoppy Hopkins at the end of 1965. Its aim was to sit at the heart of the community, offering free education through lectures and discussion groups in subjects essential to daily life and work; involved, among others, were the author George Clark, record producer Joe Boyd, poet Michael Horovitz, actress Anjelica Huston, sculptor Emily Young (who inspired the Pink Floyd song "See Emily Play"), civil rights activist Michael X, psychiatrist R. D. Laing, singer Julie Felix, and Peter Jenner, a lecturer at the London School of Economics and future manager of Pink Floyd.

In its short life, the London Free School was responsible for kick-starting the Notting Hill Carnival, developing the underground press, and providing a venue at All Saints Church Hall for the growing psychedelic scene. The first Notting Hill Fayre, as it was then called, was held in late August 1966; as the Notting Hill Carnival, it would become Europe's biggest street festival. After the Notting Hill Fayre, Hoppy organized the London Free School Sound/Light workshops, advertised as a "pop dance" featuring London's "farthest-out" group, Syd Barrett & the Pink Floyd Sound.

> " I DECLARE THAT THE BEATLES ARE MUTANTS. PROTOTYPES OF EVOLUTIONARY AGENTS SENT BY GOD, ENDOWED WITH A MYSTERIOUS POWER TO CREATE A NEW HUMAN SPECIES, A YOUNG RACE OF LAUGHING FREEMEN." Timothy Leary, 1966

This turned into a ten-gig weekly residency at All Saints Hall, during which the Pink Floyd Sound dropped the "Sound" from their name as they transformed from a regular rhythm-and-blues band into Britain's leading psychedelic group. The Hall would go on to host performances by Hawkwind, Quintessence, David Bowie (during his mime phase), the Crazy World of Arthur Brown, and musician and actor Ram John Holder, among others.

THE SUMMER BEFORE THE SUMMER OF LOVE

The summer of 1966 brought with it a series of landmarks in psychedelic music. Over in the US, Brian Wilson and the Beach Boys released *Pet Sounds*, now recognized as one of the earliest examples of psychedelic rock—and one of the greatest albums ever made—in May. A month later, Frank Zappa & the Mothers of Invention issued *Freak Out!*, which featured electronic sound effects, shifting song structures, and fuzz-guitar freak-outs. In July, the Byrds created jazz-raga fusion and acid-inspired imagery on their single "Eight Miles High," from their third album, *Fifth Dimension*. Not to be outdone, back in their London recording studio, the Beatles utilized backward guitar, dense Indian sounds, shifting time signatures, lyrics inspired by LSD trips and *The Tibetan Book of the Dead*, and Stockhausen-inspired tape loops on their new album, *Revolver*, released in August. Shortly after that, Eric Clapton, until recently the guitarist in John Mayall's Bluesbreakers, had his first encounter with Jimi Hendrix, who arrived in Britain in September. After jamming with Hendrix at a gig at the London Polytechnic in early October, Clapton immediately began to

ALL NIGHT RAVE to launch new underground newspaper 'INTERNATIONAL TIMES' the Soft Machine; the Pink Floyd; Steel Bands STRIP -TRIPS - HAPPENING MOVIE - POP - OP - COSTUME MASQUE - DRAG BALL bring your own poison, bring Flowers & Gass filled balloons SurPRIZE for Shortest & Barest at... THE ROUND HOUSE* opp. chalk farm underground SAT. 15th OCT 11 P.M. onwards advance tickets 5/- from INDICA better books; Dobells Record Shop. GRANNIE TAKE A TRIP Mandarin Book Shops at ... Nottinghill gate & Swiss Cottage, or compulsory donations of 10/- at door.

introduce psychedelic themes to his own work, resulting in *Fresh Cream*, released in December.

Back in New York, Timothy Leary formed the League for Spiritual Discovery on September 19, 1966, to advocate for the continued legal use of psychedelics for spiritual enlightenment, in the face of growing opposition across the US. Over on the West Coast, Huey Newton and Bobby Seale established the Black Panther Party on October 15, 1966, in Oakland, California, while the first issue of the underground newspaper *San Francisco Oracle*, created by the poet Allen Cohen, appeared in September.

At the same time, in London, Miles and Hoppy were finalizing plans to start a newspaper to service Britain's own

The 14-Hour Technicolor Dream

Alexandra Palace, London N22
April 29, 1967

T HE *INTERNATIONAL TIMES* was often short of the funds necessary to pay staff wages, office running costs, printers' bills, and distribution charges—expenses never fully realized by the cover price of the paper. The UFO club and various other fund-raising events such as the Common Market, held at the Roundhouse, went some way to paying the bills.

John "Hoppy" Hopkins decided that a large injection of cash was required to establish a stable fund for *IT*. At a meeting with Miles, Jim Haynes, filmmaker Jack Henry Moore, and writer David Mairowitz, he discussed the idea of a large-scale event equal to the 1965 poetry reading at the Royal Albert Hall. Hoppy suggested Alexandra Palace in North London as a venue, a great Victorian Hall built in 1875 sitting on top of Muswell Hill. The idea for holding it there came from the all-night jazz raves Hoppy had attended there as a photojournalist.

It was agreed that Hoppy would co-organize the event with Dave Howson, who went on to manage the Middle Earth club in Covent Garden. The venue was approved and booking arrangements made for a fourteen-hour event on April 29, 1967, which would become a free-speech benefit after the police raid on the *IT* offices on March 9. I was commissioned to produce the poster for the event and proceeded to prepare artwork for a silkscreen poster inking with two colors at a time to create a rainbow effect. Slugs of ink were changed throughout the printing process so that no two posters looked the same.

The Great Hall at Alexandra Palace was huge. I remember standing in the middle of the vast space as we prepared for the concert, wondering if it would fill with enough people to create the necessary atmosphere. There was no need to worry. At 8 p.m., fireworks heralded the start of the "Dream" and ten thousand people heeded the call to our night of music, poetry, dance, performance art, and large inflatables. There were two stages at either end of the hall for music and a small stage in the center for poetry reading and performance. A huge light tower in the center of the hall provided projections for light shows, strobe effects, and

ABOVE: Mike McInnerney's silkscreen poster for the 14-Hour Technicolor Dream, April 1967. No two posters looked alike as the inking was altered during printing.

RIGHT: Inside the 14-Hour Technicolor Dream, Alexandra Palace, London, April 29, 1967.

films such as Jack Smith's *Flaming Creatures*, as well as huge film arc lights turning night into day. Dudley Edwards of BEV, one of the teams providing light shows, remembers, "There was a feel of a medieval market place with stalls and people in harlequin costumes, acrobats here and jugglers there, a helter-skelter, Simon and Marijke [of The Fool] reading Tarot cards and telling fortunes in a booth. . . . It was all so relaxed, Denny Laine was just sitting on the floor, strumming his acoustic guitar with no one paying any heed." Over in one corner, Suzy Creamcheese was offering banana-skin joints, supposedly hallucinogenic and completely legal, but it didn't really matter: most people were high on the night, grooving to the

vibe, wandering aimlessly or just resting on the floor, in groups with picnics or as couples, or singly, at the edges of the hall.

John Lennon happened to be at home in Weybridge with his friend John Dunbar, on an LSD trip, when they saw live TV coverage of the event and decided to join the party. Lennon was seen wandering around as Yoko Ono's "Cut Piece" was performed to an intense group of young men. Those performing that night included Pink Floyd, the Crazy World of Arthur Brown, Soft Machine, the Move, Tomorrow, the Pretty Things, Pete Townshend, Alexis Korner, Social Deviants, the Purple Gang, Champion Jack Dupree, Graham Bond, Ginger Johnson, Gary Farr,

Ron Geesin, Mike Horovitz, Christopher Logue, Simon Vinkenoog, Dick Gregory, Yoko Ono, and many more. Pink Floyd returned straight from a gig in Holland and played in the early hours of the morning as dawn came up in what might have been a perfectly pitched inspiration for their future debut album, *The Piper at the Gates of Dawn*, released on August 5, 1967. Dudley remembers the next morning: "In the early hours people sat on the grassy bank outside the Palace, watching the dawn break. An open-backed truck drove up the hill to the entrance of the Palace; someone was stood on the back dispatching loaves of bread and bananas to all those present. Peace reigned and all was well with the world."

developing underground scene. The first issue of the *International Times* appeared on the streets of London on October 14, 1966. Hoppy and Miles had managed to put together a group of directors including Jim Haynes and Tom McGrath, who become the paper's editor. The *IT* was to be found in the basement of the relocated Indica Bookshop at 102 Southampton Row, on the fringes of Covent Garden. The front page of the first issue featured a critique of contemporary theater, while the back page carried a "happening diary"—the first notice board of events aimed directly at the alternative London scene.

The *International Times* was launched with an "All Night Rave" in Chalk Farm, Camden, at the Roundhouse (an old railroad locomotive shed) on Saturday, October 15, 1966. Tickets cost ten shillings (around $1.40 at the time) on the door for a "Pop/Op/Costume/Masque/Fantasy-Loon/Blowout/Drag Ball." Two thousand people attended to hear Soft Machine and Pink Floyd, and to witness a happening. It seemed that everyone was there, including Paul McCartney—dressed as an Arab—Jane Asher, Marianne Faithfull, and Michelangelo Antonioni with Monica Vitti, who were in town filming *Blow Up*.

The event also featured steel bands, strips, trips, and movies. The facilities were basic, with overflowing toilets and freezing conditions, but the pot-smoking, masked ball, and fancy-dress freak-show created a heady, atmosphere-warming happening that heralded the coming of alternative London.

IT soon required more long-term regular funding to cover costs, with occasional fundraising events such as the "Uncommon Market" held at the Roundhouse unable to provide stable funding. Previous concerts at All Saints Hall provided Hoppy and Joe Boyd with the idea of establishing a regular club,

with Pink Floyd and Soft Machine as house bands. (Boyd, an American record producer, would found both the Whitchseason production company and Hannibal Records and play a crucial role in the recording careers of Pink Floyd, Fairport Convention, the Incredible String Band, Sandy Denny, and Nick Drake, among others.) The proposed club would be run by *IT* staff and aimed to cover production costs for the paper and help pay staff wages.

In the fall of 1966, Boyd discovered an Irish dance hall in the basement of the Gala Berkeley Cinema on Tottenham Court Road that would cost fifteen pounds to rent for a Friday night. There was some discussion between Boyd and Hoppy regarding the naming of the club, leading to a final choice between "Nite Tripper" and "UFO," an acronym that could carry several meanings.

In the end the poster, designed by Michael English, announced the first nights on December 23 and 30, 1966, while referring to the club venue as "NiteTripper," with the words painted onto the face of Karen Astley, a designer for Hung on You and future wife of Pete Townshend. The poster presented the all-nighter as a freak-out, with Pink Floyd performing and Andy Warhol and Kenneth Anger films to be shown. Having then settled on UFO as the name for the club, Boyd brought together Michael English and Nigel Waymouth of the design partnership Hapshash & the Coloured Coat to create the next poster for Friday, January 13, 1967, a typographic design with undulating lettering in vibrant pink and orange, announcing the Sun Trolly, Kenneth Anger and Marilyn Monroe films, a Technicolor strobe, five-acre slides, karate, and food.

The UFO club was approached by a wide descending staircase, with a ticket and membership desk at the bottom of

the stairs. I would take tickets at the door and manage the *IT* stall inside the club. There was also a bar selling macrobiotic food, all supplied by Craig Sams, who went on to co-found (with his brother Greg) the Whole Earth food company, as well as the organic Green & Black's company. The first couple of nights on the ticket/membership desk were manageable, with a steady flow of people, but very soon the steady flow became a motionless crush as news about UFO spread.

The club was a place for watching people's slow-motion act of blowing bubbles moving around, high on something in a world of their own—an experience I would revisit when designing my poster for the 14-Hour Technicolor Dream at Alexandra Palace in April 1967. In the early hours of a Saturday morning, people would leave the intense iridescent bubble of UFO, climb the stairs, and stumble upon a normal day, with a deep sense of separateness as Tottenham Court Road went about its usual daily business.

PLUGGING IN
On January 14, 1967, the "Human Be-In" took place at the Polo Field in San Francisco's Golden Gate Park, a gathering of tribes and a "Peace Dance Pow-Wow" including speakers Allen Ginsberg, Timothy Leary, social activists Jerry Rubin and Dick Gregory, essayist Gary Snyder, and bookshop owner/poet Lawrence Ferlinghetti, plus bands Jefferson Airplane, the Grateful Dead, Big Brother & the Holding Company, and Quicksilver Messenger Service. The event is considered a prelude to the Summer of Love on both sides of the Atlantic, attracting a gathering of 30,000 people and popularizing the phrase "Turn on, tune in, drop out," as uttered in a speech made at the gathering by Leary. It made the Haight-Ashbury district a symbol of American counterculture and introduced the word "psychedelic" to suburbia.

News of the Human Be-In filtered through to London via the UFO club, the international news page of the *International Times* (issue 6), and airmailed copies of the *San Francisco Oracle*, as the London scene gathered pace and psychedelic culture became more visible. My new role as art editor of the *IT* would give me an insight into just how actively things were in the expanding underground.

> " THE BE-IN WAS A BLOSSOM, IT WAS A FLOWER. IT WAS OUT IN THE WEATHER. IT DIDN'T HAVE ALL ITS PETALS. THERE WERE WORMS IN THE ROSE. IT WAS PERFECT IN ITS IMPERFECTIONS. IT WAS WHAT IT WAS AND THERE HAD NEVER BEEN ANYTHING LIKE IT BEFORE." Michael McClure on the Human Be-In

OPPOSITE, FAR LEFT: A flyer for the Human Be-In or "Gathering of the Tribes" held at San Francisco's Golden Gate Park, January 14, 1967.

RIGHT: A double Paul McCartney on the cover of the *International Times*, January 1967.

OPPOSITE, LEFT: The Grateful Dead perform at the Human Be-In.

The International Times No. 6 Jan 16-29, 1967/1s.
★Paul McCARTNEY
★Norman MAILER
★William BURROUGHS
★Allen GINSBERG
★Cerebral CORTEX

The counterculture developed local, homemade, do-it-yourself alternatives to mainstream culture, leading to the creation of shops, posters, clothing, newspapers, magazines, clubs, art centers, galleries, cafés, restaurants, and centers for action, support, and debate. It adopted alternative lifestyle thinking through books such as *Architecture Without Architects* by Bernard Rudofsky, and embraced new structures for living, such as the itinerant and restless notions of inflatable structures and "plug-in city" concepts of Peter Cook—promoted in the pages of *Clip Kit* and *Archigram*—and utopian engineering ideas in the form of Buckminster Fuller's geodesic domes. And it encompassed global culture, too, with links to alternative media in Amsterdam, Berlin, New York, and San Francisco, and publications such as the *Whole Earth Catalogue*, the analog precursor of Google. Alternative global connections were created as young hitchhikers trekked individual spiritual paths to the Far East, or made personalized journeys through places like Morocco, the Middle East, and Afghanistan.

All of this was happening at a time when an increasingly paranoid establishment had begun to harbor grave concerns about the rise of the counterculture. At the Human Be-In, speakers rallied against a new law in the State of California that took effect on October 6, 1966, making LSD illegal. Governmental concerns in Britain meant that drug use had been increasingly criminalized since 1964, leading to a modification order in '66 to bring hallucinogenic substances under control, and the Dangerous Drugs Act of 1967, which gave police power to search

and detain suspected drug users. These actions were actively supported by a British tabloid press that had shown itself to be outwardly hostile to the developing counterculture, culminating in a notorious *News of the World* story, published on February 5, 1967, that accused a number of prominent musicians of taking LSD. The story led to a police raid on Keith Richards's Redlands home on February 12, 1967. Both Richards and fellow Rolling Stone Jagger, along with Robert Fraser, received court summonses for drugs offenses, with Richards and Jagger subsequently sentenced to prison—

prompting the famous London *Times* newspaper editorial by William Rees-Mogg, who asked, "Who breaks a butterfly on a wheel?" Prior to this, Hoppy Hopkins had been arrested on December 30, 1966, during a police raid on his flat in Queensway; on June 1, 1967, he was sentenced to six months in jail.

On March 9, 1967, in an establishment attempt to close down *International Times*, there was a raid by plain-clothes police officers on the Indica Bookshop and the basement offices of the paper at 102 Southampton Row. Police officers removed what they believed to be

incriminating books from the shop, including William S. Burroughs's *Naked Lunch*, and all current copies of the *IT*, as well as mailing and subscription lists and staff personal effects.

The raid effectively shut things down for the paper. On Saturday March 11, a symbolic "Death and Rise of Free Speech" wake was held for *IT* after a UFO all-nighter. At dawn, a funeral cortege, complete with full-size cardboard coffin, made its way down Whitehall to the Cenotaph war memorial, and then to Notting Hill Gate. The next day the tabloid press reported the wake as an outrage and insult to the

fallen in two world wars, missing the point of the event completely. All those involved in *IT* were nevertheless determined to publish without a break, and to find the funds to do this. Hoppy and Dave Howson were already in the process of organizing a benefit concert called the 14-Hour Technicolor Dream in order to raise funds for the paper.

The event was planned for April 19, 1967, and would be held in the vast central hall of Alexandra Palace on Muswell Hill in North London. *IT* staff decided to turn the concert into a "free-speech benefit" to create a fund for possible legal costs that might arise from the police raid. The event would be the first large occasion, after the 1965 Albert Hall poetry reading, to bring together the underground scene in one place. In the end, ten thousand people attended the all-night event.

PAINTING WITH SOUND

In an interview about the making of *Sgt. Pepper*, the Beatles' producer, George Martin, declared that "New recording techniques and electronic possibilities offered musicians the ability to paint sound rather than photograph it." This comment not only describes the Beatles' inspired process during the making of *Sgt. Pepper* but also captures something of the mood and spirit of the sixties. It suggests a personal and distinctive process usually associated with the act of painting. In contrast to the instant click of a camera button and flick of a

> "FOR THE FIRST TIME EVER, LINKING FIVE CONTINENTS AND BRINGING MAN FACE TO FACE WITH MANKIND, IN PLACES AS FAR APART AS CANBERRA AND CAPE KENNEDY, MOSCOW AND MONTREAL, SAMARKAND AND SÖDERFORS, TAKAMATSU AND TUNIS." BBC press release about the *Our World* broadcast

shutter, the performance required to paint a picture calls for improvised actions tested over time using every sense and aesthetic option to create, out of nothing, something unique. The idea of "painting sound" is appropriate for an era that saw the rise of singer/songwriters working with their own canvases of experience, improvising an audible palette of sonic tone, color, rhyme, rhythm, and melody into meaningful expression for the individual ear.

The release of *Sgt. Pepper* on June 1 provided the soundtrack to the Summer of Love, along with Procol Harum's song "A Whiter Shade of Pale," released a week earlier. On Saturday, June 2, the largest crowd ever to assemble at UFO heard Pink Floyd and their new single, "See Emily Play," with the queue at times stretching up Tottenham Court Road in central London, and the box office closing on occasions due to overcrowding. The packed audience included Jimi Hendrix and Experience bassist Chas Chandler, the Animals' Eric Burdon, Pete Townshend, and the Yardbirds.

Over on the West Coast of America, the Monterey International Pop Music Festival was held between June 16 and 18, with crowd estimates ranging from twenty-five to ninety thousand; it provided a template for the Woodstock Festival, which would come two years later. On June 25, 1967, *All You Need Is Love* was broadcast internationally via the BBC to an estimated 400 million viewers as a contribution to the *Our World* program, adding another anthem to the Summer of Love. It was the first live global television link to twenty-five countries via satellite, though it was still transmitted in black-and-white since color TV would not appear (in Britain, at least) until the end of the year.

The year 1967 was a brief iridescent moment, a shared journey, a time when the prevailing mood was one of love, and politics was made personal. That optimistic mood would not last into 1968, as angry students took to Parisian streets and politics across Europe and the United States became increasingly volatile. But though it flickered only briefly, the impact of that mood, and these times, was seismic, not least in inspiring and informing the Beatles in the writing and creation of what is widely regarded today, fifty years on, as their single greatest musical statement: *Sgt. Pepper's Lonely Hearts Club Band*.

ABOVE: An *International Times* ad listing coming attractions at the UFO, including the Move and Pink Floyd.

OPPOSITE: George Harrison, Ringo Starr, and John Lennon at their broadcast for the *Our World* program, Abbey Road, June 25, 1967.

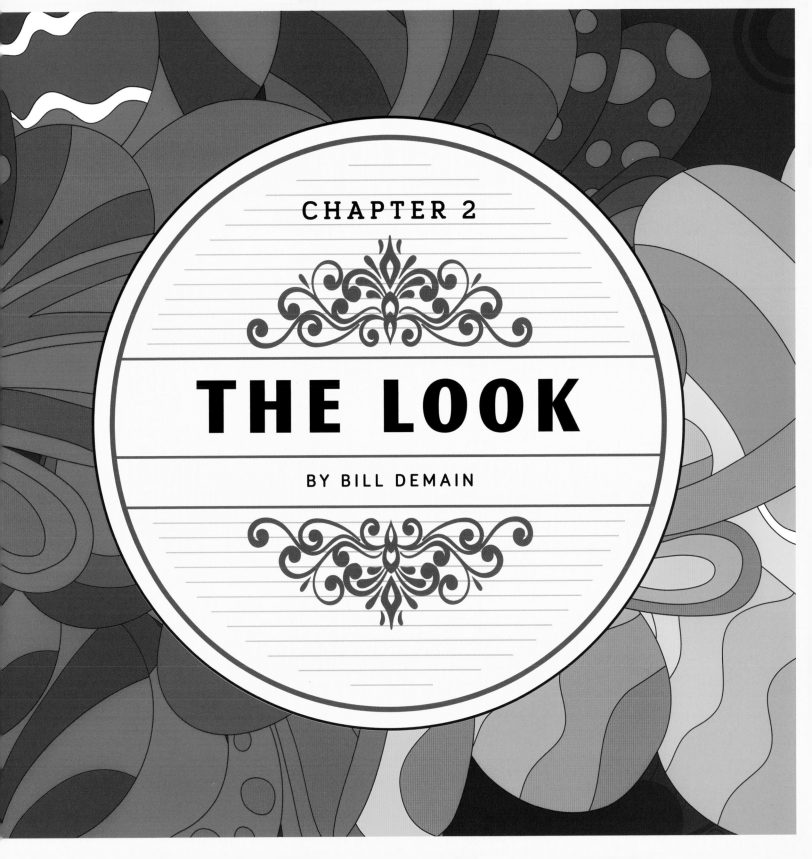

CHAPTER 2

THE LOOK

BY BILL DEMAIN

"This album was a big production, and we wanted the album sleeve to be really interesting . . . we wouldn't just have our Beatle jackets on, or we wouldn't just be suave guys in turtlenecks. . . . It would now be much more pantomime, much more 'Mr Bojangles.'"

Paul McCartney, *The Beatles Anthology*

THE BEATLES LOVED TO PLAY DRESS UP. In photo sessions early in their career, they masqueraded as Eskimos, spies, matadors, cowboys, and Shakespearean actors. Sometimes simpler disguises, like hats and glasses, helped them escape from screaming throngs of girls intent on tearing off a piece of hair or clothing as a souvenir. At the 1966 NME Awards concert, the Beatles donned chef's outfits, and, carrying trays of food, waltzed undetected past fans through the kitchen entrance of the venue.

Paul McCartney was especially fond of going incognito. On a two-day tour of Sweden in 1964, he'd slicked his hair back, put on specs and a fake mustache, grabbed a camera, and knocked on George Harrison's hotel room door, announcing in a made-up language, "Peresi, yea? Peresi?" Thinking Paul was a paparazzo, George yelled, "Piss off!" and slammed the door. The next day,

with his bandmates' encouragement, McCartney took the prank further, using the same disguise to blend in with the press pack interviewing the other three Fabs outside the hotel.

This love of costumes and artful dodgery became crucial in late 1966, when the group faced a mid-career crisis question: to Beatle or not to Beatle?

The answer was already clear. By August, they had expanded their sound with *Revolver*, weathered the American press disaster of Lennon's "bigger than Jesus" comment, and bowed out of live performance with their last-ever concert, at San Francisco's Candlestick Park. John flew off to Spain, to play Private Gripweed in Richard Lester's *How I Won the War*. George spent a month in India, studying sitar with Ravi Shankar (and was also photographed in the studio that fall wearing a sweatshirt that read, "Stamp Out the Beatles!"). Paul delved into London's avant-garde

art scene and composed the score for *The Family Way* (its "northern brass band feel" would go on to influence his thinking about *Sgt. Pepper*). And Ringo was "happily getting fat," as well as overseeing his new construction venture, Bricky Builders.

Even more significantly, all four had experimented with marijuana and LSD. Suddenly, there was a new psychedelic horizon coming into view, with vivid colors, striped trousers, backward guitars, and an ambitious soundtrack signposted by the double-A side single of "Strawberry Fields Forever" and "Penny Lane."

"We were fed up with being the Beatles," Paul McCartney said. "We really hated that fucking four little mop-top boys approach. We were not boys, we were men." They'd started smoking pot, too, and had begun to think of themselves not as mere performers but as "artists."

PREVIOUS SPREAD: The Beatles dressed up as Shakespearean actors for a TV performance, April 1964.

ABOVE: The "old" Beatles adjust their ties, January 1963.

ABOVE RIGHT: Lennon on the set of *How I Won the War*, October 5, 1966.

RIGHT: The "new" Beatles show off their new mustaches, August 1967.

Pepper Sprouts: How the Beatles' Mustaches Set Them Free in the Summer of Love

WE LIVE IN A TIME of free-flowing facial hair Mustaches and beards are everywhere. The sight of young men sporting the hirsute looks of nineteenth-century presidents and pugilists barely raises an eyebrow.

But fifty years ago, in the months before *Sgt. Pepper*, facial hair was a head-turning rarity on anyone under the age of sixty-five. Especially in Britain, cheeks, chins, and upper lips were almost unanimously bare.

The Beatles' hairdresser, Leslie Cavendish, said, "Only two kinds of people wore mustaches—spivs and old men. As soon as they started wearing them, you saw loads of people out on the street with mustaches."

George Harrison took a deeper view, saying, "Mustaches were part of the synchronicity and the collective consciousness of the time."

Whatever started them sprouting in the mid-sixties, mustaches were the accessories that allowed the Beatles to move on from their mop-top past.

Paul McCartney grew his first. Or, actually, he had a fake one made. During the *Hard Day's Night* shoot,

he asked Wig Creations, the film makeup company, to fashion a 'stache that matched his hair color. He then used it as a part of a disguise that enabled him to travel around Paris unrecognized, "retasting anonymity" during the height of Beatlemania. But Paul's first real mustache was less a fashion statement than a bit of aesthetic camouflage. In spring 1966, he fell off his moped and cut his lip and chipped his front tooth. In a photo shoot shortly after the accident, makeup and a bit of chewing gum disguised the injury, but after that Paul decided to grow a mustache to cover it up. "I was originally trying to grow a long Chinese one," he recalled, "but it was very difficult. You have to do a lot of work, waxing it, and it takes about sixty years."

George Harrison had his own personal reasons. "Ravi had written to me [prior to George's trip to Bombay to study sitar]

saying, 'Maybe you could disguise yourself? Maybe grow a mustache or something?' The idea that a mustache could be a disguise—it was all pretty naive in those days. And anyway a mustache on a Beatle was kind of 'unexpected.'" Though George checked into the Taj Mahal Hotel as Mr. Sam Wells, a bellboy saw through the mustache and news spread that a Beatle was in town.

Fashion-conscious Ringo Starr spent a lot of time in King's Road suits with interesting collars and ruffle-fronted shirts, so the mustache made an ideal Edwardian-style complement. But it was John Lennon's new handlebar mustache, along with his new wire-rimmed granny glasses (acquired as part of his onscreen look in the forties-era *How I Won the War*) that made for the most startling transformation of the group's career to date. Looking at the

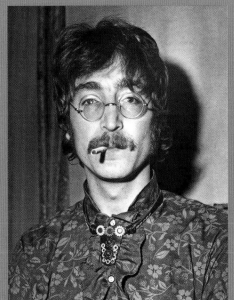

owlish professor figure he cut in 1967, it's almost impossible to recognize the singer of "Help!" from two years before. It's like some Victorian-era ancestor. Lennon took the idea even further with some 1890s-style pampering.

"John had a mustache cup," McCartney said. "It had a little hole underneath the lip so you could drink tea from it without getting your mustache in it—rather fetching."

Rather fetching too was the cutout mustache included in the album's cardboard insert, offering colorful encouragement for everyone, even pre-pubescent male fans, to be a Pepper too.

"[In 1967], it became seen as a revolutionary idea, that young men should definitely grow a mustache," McCartney said. "And it fell in with the Sgt. Pepper thing, because he had a droopy mustache."

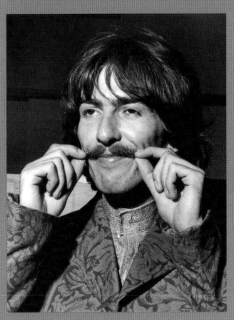

Fifty years on, this transition may not seem daunting. But a lot was at stake, and the Beatles, always pioneers, were the first pop group to ever make the effort to be taken seriously. "That was a pretty big dare and it changed everything," McCartney recalled, while John Lennon told *NME* that *Sgt. Pepper* was one of the most important steps in the band's career: "It had to be just right." What better way to make that step than with alter egos that would engage their fans on a new level while symbolically closing the chapter on Beatlemania? And so, inspired by the "jingly jangly hippie aura" and "long-named group thing" he'd observed on a recent trip to San Francisco, Paul dreamed up Sgt. Pepper's Lonely Hearts Club Band, and the Beatles slipped from Fabs into the future.

Curiously, this was a future seen through the lens of the *fin de siècle*. Mid-sixties London was a perfect time and place to be a stylish throwback, as the groovy pendulum of fashion was swinging forward and backward—from psychedelia to Victoriana. And one man who really set it swinging, appropriately, would be a prominent face on the *Sgt. Pepper* cover.

In May 1966, the V&A Museum mounted an exhibit of the works of Aubrey Beardsley. The Victorian-era artist's illustrations of well-dressed—and undressed—men and women in languidly erotic poses really captured the emerging moment of fashion and free love. Even Beardsley himself, an impeccably styled eccentric who had espoused druggy decadence and died

> **ONE'S EARS ARE WEARY OF THE VOICE OF THE ART TEACHER WHO SITS LIKE THE PARROT ON HIS PERCH, LEARNING THE JARGON OF THE STUDIOS, MAKING BUT POOR COPY AND CALLING IT CRITICISM. WE HAVE HAD ENOUGH OF THEIR OMNISCIENCE."** Aubrey Beardsley, 1894

tragically at age twenty-five, seemed like a zeitgeist pinup.

You could see the influence blooming in Day-Glo colors in window displays along London's two main fashion routes, Soho's Carnaby Street and the King's Road in Chelsea. The boutiques that had

first flourished in the early sixties as suppliers of crisply-tailored mod style were now looking like a 1899 revival, with flared trousers, velvet jackets and cloaks, neck scarves and ascots—all given a psychedelic twist with eye-popping lavenders, scarlets, and greens.

"We created a new look inspired by Beardsley, Oscar Wilde, and the Salon," said tailor John Pearse, who co-ran Granny Takes a Trip, one of the Beatles' favorite boutiques on the King's Road. "We were interested in decadence and flamboyance."

Within the turn-of-the-century fashion resurgence, the look that most informed *Sgt. Pepper* was the Edwardian. It was defined by military-style jackets and shirts with frilly fronts and fluted cuffs. As the rank in the title suggested, Pepper's was a military brass band. So of course they would wear uniforms.

The seeds for the iconic look of the Fabs' alter egos had already been planted. In 1965, at their famous Shea Stadium concert, they wore tan army-style jackets, designed by their tailor, Dougie Millings. On the ride out to the stage, the drivers of the Wells Fargo van gave the lads some authentic agent badges to pin on their jackets. A year later, Lennon was photographed for *Life* wearing a knee-length cream-colored military tunic with gold brocade. He'd bought it at another favorite boutique,

ABOVE LEFT: John Walker of the Walker Brothers at the Lord John boutique on Carnaby Street, London, 1967.

ABOVE RIGHT: The scene outside I Was Lord Kitchener's Valet on Portobello Road, another boutique that specialized in military fashions.

OPPOSITE: A print ad for the Granny Takes a Trip boutique on King's Road.

GRANNY TAKES A TRIP

EAST OF EDEN....
488 King's Road

WE WERE DEALING IN VINTAGE CLOTHES. WHAT APPEALED TO US WAS AUBREY BEARDSLEY AND THE VICTORIANS, *AGAINST NATURE* BY HUYSMANS. SO WE WERE ALL DOOMED ROMANTICS AT THE TIME. NOT NEW ROMANTICS, DOOMED ROMANTICS. SO THAT WAS THE INFLUENCE—ART NOUVEAU." John Pearse, cofounder of Granny Takes a Trip

I Was Lord Kitchener's Valet (named for Herbert Kitchener, a decorated and mustachioed World War I hero who looked like he could've pulled rank on Sgt. Pepper), which specialized in antique military clothes. As Lennon later said, "Kids were already wearing army jackets on the King's Road. All we did was make them famous."

Carnaby Street and King's Road aside, for bespoke military gear, there was only one name in London—Monty Berman. His company, M. Berman, Ltd., based in Leicester Square, was a world-renowned costumer for film, TV, and theater that put the costume in costume dramas such as *Lawrence of Arabia*, *Cleopatra*, and *The Guns of Navarone*. The firm,

started in the late eighteenth century by Berman's great-grandfather, had also tailored uniforms for the royal family. During World War II, it worked with the British Army to create authentic-looking Nazi uniforms for an espionage mission behind German lines. And though it clothed everyone from Eliza Doolittle to Vegas showgirls, military garb was the company's specialty.

Berman first sent a rep to EMI Studios with some bright fabric swatches. Appetites whetted, the Beatles took an afternoon to romp through Berman's warehouse, where their imaginations "went wild," as McCartney later put it. At the time, Berman's was the place to go for film costumes and was equipped with books showing the range of styles available. The Beatles ended up going for a mishmash of "oddball" items in a range of psychedelic hues. "At the back of our minds, I think the plan was to have garish uniforms which would actually go *against* the idea of uniforms," McCartney recalled. "At the time everyone was into that Lord Kitchener's thing, kids in bands wearing soldier's outfits and putting flowers in the barrels of rifles."

To the uniforms, Paul, George, and Ringo would add their own flourishes,

including the red-ribboned MBE medals they'd been awarded in 1965. But John's tunic had some extra brass, thanks to decorations from ex-drummer Pete Best's grandfather, Major Thomas Shaw. Lennon, a fan of military paraphernalia, remembered the medals long after Best had been replaced. They were awarded to Shaw for exemplary service with the British Raj in India. Lennon called Best's mother, Mona, and asked if he could borrow the medals for the photo shoot. They were sent to London, then returned afterward, with a thank you note and a copy of *Pepper*.

As the Beatles were getting fitted at Berman's, they were brainstorming about how to best frame their new alter egos on an LP cover. "We thought, 'Let's find roles for these people,'" McCartney said. Rock's most iconic—and elaborately staged—album sleeve is made even more remarkable by how quickly it came together. While the music for *Sgt. Pepper* required nearly five months in the studio—an unprecedented length in the three-songs-a-day sixties—the equally complex artwork, from first idea to final touch-up, took a mere five weeks.

And, like many great endeavors, it almost didn't happen.

FIXING A HOLE

By late February 1967, McCartney had made some rough pen-and-ink sketches for a cover concept. His first inspiration was a 1920s-era photo of his father's orchestra, Jim Mac's Jazz Band, surrounded by their well-dressed dance club fans. To that, he wove in fond childhood memories of Northern brass bands playing outdoor events in parks.

"I did a lot of drawings of us being presented to the Lord Mayor," Paul said, "with dignitaries and friends of ours around, and it was to be us in front of a big northern floral clock, and we were to look like a brass band. The idea was to have these guys in their new identity, in their costumes, being presented with the 'Freedom of the City.' We always liked to take those ordinary facts of northern working-class life, like the clock, and mystify them and glamorize them and make them into something more magical, more universal."

Meanwhile, Paul was fielding ideas from his art-scene friends. "Everyone was throwing in their two-penny worth," he said. Gallery owner John Dunbar, who was married to Marianne Faithfull, suggested an abstract picture without

ABOVE LEFT: A fireplace painted by The Fool at Kinfauns, George Harrison's home in Esher, Surrey.

ABOVE RIGHT: The Apple Boutique on Baker Street, London, prior to its grand opening on December 7, 1967.

OPPOSITE, LEFT: The Dutch design collective The Fool at the Apple Building, 1967.

OPPOSITE, RIGHT: Harrison takes a break from a game of Monopoly to chat to right-hand man Neil Aspinall.

text or explanation, but Paul thought that too experimental. Paul also invited Simon Posthuma and Marijke Koger, better known as The Fool, to do a painting for the album.

After relocating to London in 1966, the Dutch duo had made a name for themselves designing colorful costumes for the Hollies and the Move, and brushing psychedelic swirls onto everything from Carnaby Street storefronts to John Lennon's upright piano. They fell into Beatleworld after Brian Epstein hired them to design programs for a concert series he was promoting at the Saville Theatre. The Fool were "part of our crowd," as Paul put it. They would also make clothes for the band, and painted a mural on the façade of the Apple Boutique on Baker Street. The painting—a trippy landscape cluttered with peacocks, owls, and stars flying around a magic mountain—was very typical of the time, an acid-inspired fantasy. But it had problems that were more down to earth.

The Beatles' right-hand man, Neil Aspinall, recalled, "They hadn't somehow checked on the album size and their design was just out of scale. So they said, 'Oh, okay, we'll put a border on it.' So we now had a design which was too small and a border being added just to fill up space. I said to the fellows, 'What are we selling here, a Beatles album or a centerfold with a design by The Fool which isn't even ready?'"

> " I WAS SO BUSY THERE WAS NO TIME FOR ANY OTHER CLIENTS. . . . WE PAINTED MURALS IN THEIR HOMES, DESIGNED CLOTHES FOR THEM PERSONALLY, THEN WERE COMMISSIONED TO DESIGN THE OUTFITS FOR THEIR 'ALL YOU NEED IS LOVE' LIVE TELECAST." Marijke Koger of The Fool

Aspinall wasn't even its most vocal critic. While there's been some dispute about whether The Fool's work was intended for the cover or the gatefold, what matters most is that it became the catalyst for a new approach to album art.

Who's Who on the Cover

> **"I**T'S A BIG THING being on a Beatle cover.
> I would think they would be pleased."

That was Paul McCartney in late May 1967, blithely reassuring EMI president Sir Joseph Lockwood, who'd come to McCartney's house to express concern over how the label would soon be "up to their eyeballs in lawsuits" with so many famous people on the cover. One of those, Mahatma Gandhi, was a definite no-go. "Sir Joe said it could be taken as an insult in India," Paul said.

To further his case, Lockwood had even brought a mock-up version of the sleeve minus the crowd, with the Beatles standing in front of a blue sky. Manager Brian Epstein had also been against the crowd concept from the beginning but was swayed when he saw how striking it was. Now, with a week before the release and the Beatles unwilling to compromise, Epstein enlisted his long-suffering assistant, Wendy Hanson, to secure permissions from each person or their estate.

"I spent many hours and pounds on calls to the States," Hanson recalled. "Some people agreed to it, but others wouldn't. Fred Astaire was very sweet and Shirley Temple wanted to hear the record first. I got on famously with Marlon Brando, but Mae West wanted to know what she would be doing in a lonely hearts club." In the end, Hanson and EMI ran out of time.

Amazingly, there has never been a single legal claim, even though the Beatles didn't bother to contact everybody. As compared to today, the sixties were probably less litigious, but it was more part of the magic of the Beatles that everybody was glad to be along, with "a splendid time guaranteed for all."

HEARTS CLUB A–Z

FRED ASTAIRE (9) McCartney always had a fondness for the legendary song-and-dance man, paying tribute on Wings' "You Gave Me the Answer" and his solo album *Kisses on the Bottom*.
MAHAVATAR BABAJI (26) An Indian saint, he appeared again on George's *Dark Horse* album cover.
AUBREY BEARDSLEY (15) A Victorian-era eccentric artist whose illustrations and personal style inspired 1967's fashions.
BEATLES WAXWORKS (53–56) Peter Blake said, "It made absolute sense that the Beatles could be fans of *Sgt. Pepper*. It didn't occur to me that the waxworks looked like 'The Beatles are dead; long live the Beatles.' And that they were looking at their funeral flowers. But it's an interesting idea."
LARRY BELL (42) Another favorite of Blake's, Bell is an American artist known for his abstract paintings and shadowboxes.
WALLACE BERMAN (22) The father of "assemblage," a 3D collage that influenced Blake and Haworth. Berman was also one of the first fine artists to design album covers, working for jazz artists such as Charlie Parker.
ISSY BONN (46) "The Famous Hebrew Comedian," Bonn also had a tenor made for gramophones. His figure is waving, which placed his hand above Paul's head—a coincidence that later got reinterpreted as an omen in the "Paul Is Dead" controversy.

MARLON BRANDO (38) The method actor had a strange connection to the Fabs. In his 1953 film *The Wild One* (as he's pictured), there's a scene where he gets in a scuffle with Lee Marvin, and Marvin motions to his gang, saying, "We missed you, Johnny, the beetles missed ya, all the beetles missed ya."
BOBBY BREEN (58) Singing child star in 1930s Hollywood.
LENNY BRUCE (4) An apt companion for Mae West, the candid Bruce's mining of his stormy personal life for material influenced generations of comedians.
WILLIAM S. BURROUGHS (25) Paul was so impressed by Burroughs' spoken word album *Call Me Burroughs* that he hired its producer, Ian Sommerville, to set up a demo studio in London. It was there that Burroughs heard Paul writing "Eleanor Rigby." Burroughs said, "I could see that he knew what he was doing."
LEWIS CARROLL (50) The English writer of *Alice in Wonderland* was a great influence on Lennon's work, both as a writer of prose and songs.
STEPHEN CRANE (45) Writer of *The Red Badge of Courage*, he died of tuberculosis at twenty-eight.

ALEISTER CROWLEY (2) Occultist and early drug experimenter Crowley was a touchstone for musicians including David Bowie and Jimmy Page.
TONY CURTIS (21) The screen idol said he was "so thrilled when he found he was on the cover that he bought a dozen copies of the album" and handed them out like cigars from a proud papa.
MARLENE DIETRICH (59) The Beatles shared the stage with Dietrich at the 1963 Royal Variety Performance. Ringo said, "I remember staring at her legs—which were great."

DION DiMUCCI (20) The only other rock musician in the crowd besides Bob Dylan. He would later work with Phil Spector in the same era as Lennon.

DIANA DORS (62) The waxwork of the screen siren, minus arms and legs, sold in auction for $45,000 in 2009.

BOB DYLAN (14) One Mary Jane was the cause of it all . . . you could argue that without the joint that Dylan passed to the Fabs in 1964, *Sgt. Pepper* might never have been in their future.

right in with Pablo Fanque's Fair. A vaudeville star, he could sing, dance, and juggle.

HUNTZ HALL (12) As the slow-witted "Sach" Jones, Hall starred in fifty Bowery Boys flicks. His co-star, Leo Gorcey, was to occupy the space to his right but was removed after his agent demanded $500 for his appearance.

TOMMY HANDLEY (23) The Scouse comedian-singer, best known for his BBC radio series *It's That Man Again*, was before the Beatles' time, but he helped put Liverpool on the map.

OLIVER HARDY (29) The rotund comedian ended up in the lyric of the Wings hit "Junior's Farm."

ALDOUS HUXLEY (17) Huxley was in vogue in the Summer of Love for his 1954 book *The Doors of Perception*, an account of trips on mescaline.

CARL JUNG (7) The psychotherapist proposed "individuation"—exploring one's inner self as the path toward becoming the person you're uniquely capable of becoming. Or, as George sang, "Try to realize it's all within yourself."

STAN LAUREL (27) Another fellow Scouser, the legendary comedian was born in Lancashire County, not far from where the Beatles grew up.

T. E. LAWRENCE (51) Archaeologist and author whose experiences inspired the 1962 film *Lawrence of Arabia*.

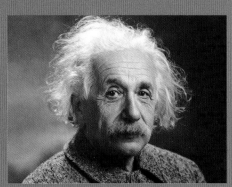

ALBERT EINSTEIN (57) It's a good thing the physicist had a famous head of hair, because that's all that's visible of him.

W. C. FIELDS (6) Though best remembered for his wisecracking "tippler" persona, Fields would've fit

RICHARD LINDNER (28) The German-born painter's blocky, brightly colored figures look like a prototype for the animated characters of *Yellow Submarine*.

SONNY LISTON (52) Maybe the oddest choice, given that the Beatles had met and posed famously with Muhammad Ali, who twice defeated Liston. Also, after attending a Beatles concert in 1964, Liston said of Ringo, "My dog drums better than that guy."

DAVID LIVINGSTONE (43) Scottish explorer and missionary, famous for his nineteenth-century travels through Africa.

KARL MARX (30) Lennon would later compare his song "Imagine" to the *Communist Manifesto*. But though he liked Marx's ideas, he said, "I'm not particularly a Communist and I do not belong to any movement."

RICHARD MERKIN (10) A natural for the *Pepper* crowd, Merkin was not only a painter of dreamy, romantic images, but also a dandy who designed his own bespoke clothes.

MAX MILLER (36) British Music Hall comedian, nicknamed the "Cheeky Chappie," sang innuendo-laced songs like "Let's Have a Ride on Your Bicycle," which was banned by the BBC.

TOM MIX (39) Silent movie actor, best known for westerns.

MARILYN MONROE (24) In one of Paul's original sketches for the cover, Brigitte Bardot was larger than any other figure. In the end, Marilyn and Brit bombshell Diana Dors replaced her. Maybe it was Lennon's disappointing encounter with Bardot in Paris. He said, "I was on acid and she was on her way out."

SIR ROBERT PEEL (16) "What's all this then?" The nineteenth-century government official who established the British police force and earned them the nickname first of "Peelers," then the more lasting "Bobbies."

PETTY GIRL (37) Illustrator George Petty, known for his long-legged pin-up girls, drew for *Esquire* and *True*.

EDGAR ALLAN POE (8) The macabre writer/poet has the distinction of being the only crowd member actually mentioned in a Beatles song ("I Am the Walrus.")

TYRONE POWER (41) Swashbuckling matinee idol of the 1940s.

SIMON RODIA (13) Peter Blake chose the Italian sculptor Rodia, best known for building the Watts Towers in Los Angeles.

GEORGE BERNARD SHAW (47) The Irish playwright once said, "Animals are my friends, and I don't eat my friends." Years later, it could've been a credo for Paul and Linda McCartney.

TERRY SOUTHERN (19) The satirist was a friend of the Beatles and later gave Ringo a starring role in *The Magic Christian*.
KARLHEINZ STOCKHAUSEN (5) The Beatles' favorite avant-garde composer influenced "Tomorrow Never Knows" and "A Day in the Life."

ALBERT STUBBINS (49) John's choice, not because of his skills as a Liverpool footballer, but because of his funny name. Indeed, Stubbins sounds like he would've fit in one of John's books, alongside Mr. Boris Morris or Eric Hearble.

STUART SUTCLIFFE (34) The original Fifth Beatle, who John called his "alter ego," died of a brain aneurysm at age twenty-two.

SHIRLEY TEMPLE (60) The former child star's image appears twice—in the front as a cloth doll and as the small figure next to Diana Dors.

DYLAN THOMAS (18) The hard-drinking, chain-smoking, womanizing Welsh writer, often called "the first rock 'n' roll poet," inspired both John Lennon and Bob Dylan.
UNKNOWN LEGIONNAIRE (61)
VARGAS GIRL (11) The Peruvian artist Alberto Vargas designed posters for the Ziegfeld Follies, then made his name creating iconic World War II–era pinups.
WAX MODELS (33, 35) Two of these were borrowed from a beauty salon.
JOHNNY WEISSMULLER (44) Olympic champion swimmer and Hollywood's most famous Tarzan.

H. G. WELLS (31) The writer of sci-fi and speculative prose foresaw television, sexual freedom, the atom bomb, and the Internet.

MAE WEST (3) The sexpot only agreed to be on the cover after all four Beatles wrote her a personal letter.
H. C. WESTERMANN (48) An American artist whose work took satirical jabs at religion, war, and politics.
OSCAR WILDE (40) The Victorian-era writer became a gay icon and sartorial inspiration for Swingin' London.
PARAMAHANSA YOGANANDA (32) His *Autobiography of a Yogi* about the search for spiritual enlightenment inspired everyone from Gandhi to Steve Jobs.
SRI YUKTESWAR GIRI (1) George's request. Yukteswar was a scholar whose book *The Holy Science* said, "There is an essential unity in all religions." In other words, all you need is love.

MISCELLANEOUS PROPS
- Cloth old lady figure by Jann Haworth
- Cloth figure of Shirley Temple by Jann Haworth (*pictured right, with the artist*)
- Mexican candlestick
- Lennon's portable TV
- Stone figure of girl
- Stone figure
- Head bust from Lennon's house
- Trophy
- Four-armed Indian doll
- Drumhead
- Hookah pipe
- Velvet snake
- Japanese stone figure
- Stone figure of Snow White
- Garden gnome
- Tuba

WHATEVER THE OTHERS SAY IS FINE BY ME." Ringo Starr, on being asked if he wanted to suggest any names for the cover

> **"I REMEMBER ROBERT FRASER BRINGING PAUL MCCARTNEY TO MY STUDIO ONCE AND THE TWO OF THEM SEEING WONDERFUL REDS AND GREENS THAT I DIDN'T REALIZE WERE THERE!"** Peter Blake

It started when Paul shared his brass band sketches and The Fool's painting with gallery owner friend Robert Fraser. An Eton-educated art prodigy and bon vivant who'd lived in Paris and opened what became London's hippest gallery in 1962, "Groovy Bob" was something of a butterfly collector, netting the beautiful and talented. Into his drug-fueled orbit came the likes of the model and actress Twiggy, the photographer David Bailey, the sculptor Claes Oldenburg, and, later, the graffiti artist Keith Haring.

Fraser loved Paul's sketches but he loathed the painting and insisted the band ditch it. "It's not good art," he said. McCartney resisted at first but eventually deferred to the wisdom of a man he later described as having "one of the greatest visual eyes I've ever met" and took up Fraser's suggestion of working instead with two of his clients, Peter Blake and Jann Haworth, and their friend, the photographer Michael Cooper.

Blake and Haworth were a married couple, both successful, with a love of Pop Art's nostalgia, advertising, and celebrity-culture imagery. Blake was thirty-five years old, English, reserved —a compact man with a pointy beard and a playful sense of humor. In *Pop Goes the Easel*, a 1959 BBC documentary directed by Ken Russell, Blake was introduced as the leader of the British Pop Art movement. There he was, cavorting with midget clowns at a carnival and at home, dreaming beneath a blanket covered with a collage of nineteenth-century military men, and painting in his studio, the walls pinned with photos of Kim Novak and the Everly Brothers.

Ten years his junior, Haworth was American, the pert, lively daughter of a Hollywood set designer who grew up around Marlon Brando and Tony Curtis. She describes her teenage years as a mix of "hot dogs, rodeos, and striped toothpaste." An early pioneer of soft sculpture and installations, she was also "obsessed with fairground art."

The mesh of personalities and artistic approaches made Blake and Haworth ideal collaborators for the Beatles' retro-future journey, and both would help give the cover its breadth and character.

McCartney recalled his first meeting with the couple in their very ordinary "little suburban house," piled up like an antiques shop with art by Blake and others: tattooed ladies, collages, pinups, and more. While the three chatted about common interests, like Gene Vincent and Elvis, Paul explored the house. Two of Haworth's waxwork dummies were on the settee. A recent show at Fraser's gallery had been a collection of her oversized teddy bears, each wearing British poet John Betjeman's face. Appropriately, Betjeman was known for his poems that celebrated English suburbia. Haworth had the teddy bears in a drawing room filled with potted plants. Paul must've felt like he'd stepped into Sgt. Pepper's waiting room.

With Fraser along for encouragement, the three met again at EMI Studios, then at Paul's place, to listen to some unfinished tracks. As Blake later told *MOJO*, "My contribution at that point was to imagine the Beatles had just finished a concert in a bandstand in a park, and were being applauded by a crowd of their fans, who could be this magic crowd. If the crowd could be made via existing photography," he thought, "anybody could be depicted, from Jesus onward. To me, it wasn't an arrogant idea, it was a magical idea.

"The appeal of a crowd for me goes back to being a young kid, as a football fan," Blake continued. "I'd painted a scene of a battle, where there was a balcony at the top and famous people looking over it, such as W. C. Fields.

ABOVE LEFT: Peter Blake emerges from his studio, a bike shed at the bottom of his parents' garden in Dartford, January 1958.

ABOVE RIGHT: West End art gallery director Robert Fraser, June 1967.

LEFT: Marianne Faithfull at one of Fraser's gallery openings.

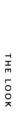

These were *Sgt. Pepper's* antecedents. I'd worked in crowds, with a series of circus collages, and the crowd made up of whatever I could find, like bits of engraving or photos."

Haworth says, "Concept two came up at this time, that the crowd was the Beatles' heroes—and that too was something that Peter had used in his teaching prior to 1967."

To help them get into character as Sgt. Pepper's band, the Beatles started to think about who their heroes might be. "Who would my character admire?"

McCartney wondered. They put together a diverse list—everyone from Marlon Brando to Albert Einstein—and started whittling it down. "All George wanted was Maharishis," Blake recalled. "And Ringo said, 'Whatever the lads want, that's fine.'" According to McCartney, "John wanted Hitler and Jesus, which was John just wanting to be bold and brassy. I didn't agree with it, but he was just trying to be far out."

Haworth agrees. "Hitler was John's misguided choice. We made the figure but removed him before the shoot. But

ABOVE LEFT: Jann Haworth at the home in Chiswick, London, she shared with husband and collaborator Peter Blake.

ABOVE RIGHT: Haworth and Blake relax at home in the late sixties.

RIGHT: Blake puts his feet up in his Chiswick garden, 1963.

FAR RIGHT: Haworth at the other end of the garden with two of her soft sculptures, circa 1965. The "Old Lady" figure on the right features on the cover of *Sgt. Pepper*.

> **" I WAS WORKING CLASS, AND BROUGHT A DIFFERENT CULTURE INTO FINE ART. I WAS LIVING WITH MY MUM IN GRAVESEND AND WE'D BE GOING TO THE WRESTLING ONCE A WEEK AND SEEING THE WEST HAM SPEEDWAY TEAM, SO I BROUGHT SPORT AND FAIRGROUNDS AND MUSIC HALL AND JAZZ WITH ME. THAT'S WHERE MY POP ART CAME FROM— AUTOBIOGRAPHICAL POPULAR CULTURE."** Peter Blake

in the end, the Beatles only selected about one-third of the heads on the cover, so Peter and I chose the rest. I wish there'd been more women represented and that I had used my education to cite some individuals of greater interest: Sherwood Anderson, Mother Jones, Ella Fitzgerald. All of these and more were in my range of interests. But our world view then was still pretty slim."

As the list grew beyond sixty names, Blake was still toying with the idea of doing the cover as a straight collage,

then Haworth had the inspiration to stage it as a life-sized set. "This was part of my movie thinking," she says. "I'd done installations. The idea of the front row being three-dimensional, leading into a two-dimensional flat frame was very much the territory of my work."

Meanwhile, Jann's dad, Ted Haworth, a production designer for films like *Marty* and *Some Like It Hot*, was in London that spring, working on *Half a Sixpence*, and Jann solicited his advice. "He suggested a backlit transparency, but we couldn't afford it.

So I went out to Pinewood [the British movie studio] to see how Dad had made a park—similar to the album concept— out of a soundstage. Interestingly, the centerpiece for the park was a merry- go-round painted by Joe Ephgrave, who did the Pepper drumhead. I'd put my Dad in touch with Joe when he said he was looking for a merry-go-round for *Half a Sixpence*."

Facing budgetary and time limits, Blake and Haworth decided to create the illusion of an outdoor park, using blue paper for the sky, and black-and-

> **I TALKED TO THE BEATLES AT LENGTH ABOUT WHAT THE COVER WOULD BE. I WORKED OUT IT WOULD SHOW THE MOMENT AFTER THEY HAD PLAYED IN A BANDSTAND IN THE PARK. MY BIG CONTRIBUTION WAS THE LIFE-SIZE CUTOUTS, THE MAGIC CROWDS."** Peter Blake

white cutout photographs for the magic crowd. The job of assembling the crowd photos was handed off to Gene Mahon, an ad man hired as coordinator on the project (and also the man who later created the famous Apple logo). His trusty gofers, Neil Aspinall and Beatle roadie Mal Evans, were sent to scour libraries for books and magazines. In came images of strange bedfellows like Aleister Crowley, Marlene Dietrich, Oscar Wilde, and Laurel & Hardy. The enlargements were made quickly, glued to hardboard (aka Masonite) sheets and then sent on to Haworth for "staining with photo ink color."

Screen idol Tyrone Power was the first one she tinted, and the Caucasian skin tone was a "really orange" shade. "He is really tan!" Haworth says with a laugh. "I got marginally better as I progressed through them."

THE SHOOT
At the end of March, Blake and Haworth—plus Aspinall, Evans, and three assistants—worked for eight days, building the set in Michael Cooper's photographic studio at Chelsea Manor Studios, Flood Street, in Kensington. (The rental fee plus overtime, since it ran into Easter weekend, was £625.)

They fixed the top row of the crowd to the back wall then put the next about six inches in front, and so on, to create the tiered effect. The total depth of the crowd behind the Beatles is surprisingly only two feet. "Again, that's an old movie trick," says Haworth.

Waxwork dummies of Sonny Liston (who was about to be melted down, since he wasn't world champ anymore), Diana Dors, and the early Beatles, borrowed from Madame Tussauds, took their places in front, while the old lady and Shirley Temple dolls were Haworth's art pieces she brought in. The Rolling Stones T-shirt on the former belonged to Michael Cooper's young son Adam—a gift from the band, as Michael regularly shot the Stones. A palm tree filled a gap on the left, and various other objects belonging to the band were scattered elsewhere (see page 77). John Lennon brought his portable TV set (a nine-inch Sony— a pretty advanced piece of home gadgetry for 1967), and a head bust from his mantelpiece. Paul's preferred objects were brass band instruments, so he rented a vanload of French horns, trumpets, and tubas. George Martin would later say, "They wanted to have these very un-Beatle instruments in the

photo. The only trouble is, they didn't know how to hold them."

For the front of the set, flower orders were placed with Clifton Nurseries—one of London's oldest, established in 1851. Haworth says, "I didn't want a graphic designer to come in and slap on lettering as they thought fit over the cover. I wanted to control that, so suggested that we do a sort of civic floral bed, with 'The Beatles,' and the album title displayed on the drumhead."

"The boy who delivered the floral display asked if he could contribute by making a guitar out of hyacinths," Blake later recalled. "It was such a nice gentle sweet sort of idea that we said, 'Yes, certainly.'"

"It's so stupid, it doesn't even look like a guitar," Haworth says. "It looks like a bone or something. And those zany hyacinths. What I wanted was tight, low-potted plants so that the entire dirt area was covered and the lettering was close to the ground. What I got were these perpendicular, absurd hyacinths. It was so far from the original concept I had in my head. I wanted it to look like the civic garden display at Hammersmith that I passed every time I went into town. What I got to work with was like working with pink celery stalks."

Fairground Attraction: The Mystery of the Drumhead

IF YOU GOOGLE "JOE EPHGRAVE," you'll find a few entries connected to the Beatles, but nothing about the man himself. For one who designed the world's most famous drumhead, Ephgrave has remained an enigma.

"Did he even exist?" asks one of the entries, imagining his name was short for "Eptitaph-Grave"—and yet another clue in the "Paul Is Dead" trail.

"Joe definitely existed," says Jann Haworth. "He was my friend, a fairground painter. And I was obsessed with fairground painting. My dad gave me a camera and taught me to use it and I was something of a fairground groupie. I took hundreds of photographs of fairground equipment at the time. Joe would advise me where Anderson Gallopers [carousel horses] were going to be in the ever-moving landscape of British fairgrounds at the time. He also painted two wardrobes and a hall stand for me. He lived in a caravan in Beaches Yard, out west of London."

In keeping with the Beatles' notion of a Northern brass band, Haworth had the idea that they should have a personalized bass drumhead.

"Joe and I talked about his futuristic style and old-fashioned style," says Haworth of the iconic lettering. "And I said I thought a bit of both would be good. He did two versions of the drumhead. I think he was paid twenty-five pounds."

As striking as his artwork was, Ephgrave did make one small grammatical error. "There should be an apostrophe between the r and the s on the drum," says Haworth. "It is 'Sgt. Pepper's Lonely Hearts Club Band,' not 'Sgt. Peppers,' as if his name is 'Peppers.' I wish we could've fixed that."

And what happened to the two drumheads? The one from the sleeve belonged to John Lennon for a few years after *Sgt. Pepper*, then changed hands a few times before being auctioned at Christie's in 2008 for one million dollars. Paul McCartney owns the alternate head.

And what about the mysterious Mr. Ephgrave?

"Someone said he went to Australia," says Haworth. "I was looking for his kids once online and came across an entry by a granddaughter. I think that unpacked a bit of a story. But to see how much Joe's design has been copied—it breaks your heart. Oh well . . . "

"THE DRUM, BY THE WAY, WAS PART OF MY THOUGHTS TO AVOID THE DREADED IMPOSITION OF LETTERING BY A GRAPHIC DESIGNER." Jann Haworth

BELOW LEFT: Joe Ephgrave's initial sketches for a design he painted onto a wardrobe for Haworth, details of which echo his work for the *Sgt. Pepper* cover.

BELOW RIGHT: One of the two *Pepper* drumheads, which sold at auction for one million dollars in 2008.

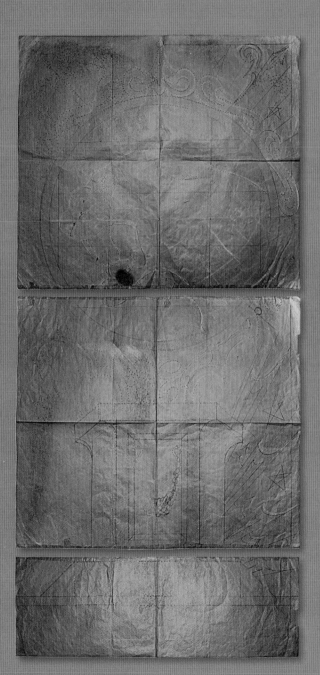

LEFT: The Madame Tussauds waxworks of the Beatles and Diana Dors used on the cover of *Sgt. Pepper*.

The plants along the front border of the rostrum, with their pointed oval-shaped leaves, would later raise speculation. "People think they're pot plants, but they're not," McCartney later noted. "It was all straight."

The floral deliveries had been nursed in a hothouse to guarantee peak bloom for the day of the photo shoot, March 29. But at the last minute, the Beatles pushed the session back a day to allow them to add fairground sound effects to "Being for the Benefit of Mr. Kite!" So everything went back in the fridge.

Finally, on March 30, 1967, at around 3 p.m., with the magic crowd awaiting, John, Paul, George, and Ringo arrived for the shoot. "We had a drink," Blake said, "they got dressed and we did the session. It took about three hours in all, including the shots for the centerfold and back cover."

"It was thoughtful and quiet," Haworth says. "Michael directed the action, having them try different poses around the drum. But the Beatles had plenty of camera experience by then."

Fraser pushed for the gatefold's large portrait shot, still angling to eliminate The Fool's painting. "Robert said, 'No, you've got to have these four big pictures, it's the only way,'" McCartney recalled. "'You've got a busy cover. You've turned your backs there, you've got all the lyrics, all these inserts. You've got to have four big, powerful images. 'No, we want another fiddly little acid-y drawing.' So he was very helpful."

ABOVE LEFT: Jann Haworth's "Old Lady" doll, dressed for the *Sgt. Pepper* cover in a Rolling Stones t-shirt that belonged to Michael Cooper's son Adam.

ABOVE MIDDLE: Max Miller's shoes and stick, as displayed at Peter Blake's London home alongside the cutout of Miller that appears on the cover.

ABOVE RIGHT: John Lennon's Lonely Hearts Club Band suit.

> **I TOLD THEM THEY WOULD HAVE TO TAKE GANDHI OUT AS HE WAS A HOLY MAN AND THAT THEY WOULD HAVE TO GET PERMISSION FROM EACH OF THE PEOPLE INCLUDED IN THE PICTURE BEFORE WE WOULD AGREE TO ITS USE."** Sir Joseph Lockwood, chairman of EMI

If there's a vestige of the mop-top Beatles, it's the portrait. Behind the uniforms and mustaches, you can still see the boyish twinkle. "One of the things we were very much into in those days was eye messages," McCartney said. "So with Michael's inside photo, we all said, 'Now look into this camera and really say, I love you! Really try and feel love; really give love through this! It'll show.' . . . And that's what that is, if you look at it, you'll see the big effort from the eyes."

With the shoot wrapped, the Beatles returned to Abbey Road, where, in the spirit of things, they spent the night recording "With a Little Help from My Friends."

FANTABULASTICOUS!

On May 19, Brian Epstein hosted a launch party for journalists and noted disc jockeys like Kenny Everett and Jimmy Savile. Photos show the Beatles in psychedelic gear, displaying the cover with obvious pride.

Turn Me on, Policeman: How a Badge Helped Start a Conspiracy

EVERYWHERE THEY TOURED, the Beatles were showered with presents. From keys to the city to homemade cards to jelly beans, they were on the receiving end of more fan love than they could possibly keep. But one gift made it onto the *Pepper* cover and helped fuel the "Paul Is Dead" conspiracy.

After a concert in Toronto in 1966, as the group was being driven to the airport in a police van, John Lennon was given a patch that said O.P.P.—Ontario Provincial Police. Lennon loved badges and medals, so he kept it. Later, it got sewn onto the left sleeve of Paul's uniform. In the gatefold photo, the patch is partially obscured, so clue-hunting fans later read it as O.P.D., or "Officially Pronounced Dead."

"It's all bloody stupid," Paul told *Life magazine* in 1969, after they tracked him down on holiday in Scotland. "It's a police badge."

Rumors of Paul's death first started in 1967, after his Mini Cooper was involved in a crash. But Paul wasn't even in the car. He'd lent it to Robert Fraser's assistant, Mohammed Hadjij, to run an errand. Hadjij was banged up, but not seriously hurt. Still, stories circulated that Paul had been killed, and the Beatles quietly replaced him with a lookalike, soundalike double.

Tragedy aside, it would have been quite some feat.

Two years later, a Detroit DJ named Russ Gibb stirred up the story again, playing a section of "Revolution 9" backward, supposedly revealing the phrase "Turn me on, dead man." And there began a conspiracy that has lingered to this day.

As obsessive fans pored over albums and songs for clues, *Sgt. Pepper* yielded ten more:

1 The floral arrangement in front is for a funeral, and the white flowers at the bottom right, either form the shape of a left-handed bass, or they spell "Paul?"

2 The floral heart-and-arrow after "Beatles" could be an *o*, spelling "Be At Leso," a coded message about "Leslo," the Greek Island the band nearly bought in 1967 and its role in the mystery. A burial ground?

3 A small Aston Martin sits on the lap of the Rolling Stones doll at the right of the crowd—a reference to the car accident.

4 The hand over Paul's head symbolizes death, as if he were being blessed by a priest. Though the hand was attached to the figure of Issy Bonn, some believed it belonged to the man behind him, Stephen Crane, an author who died in his twenties and once wrote a story, "The Open Boat," about surviving a shipwreck.

5 If you hold a mirror across the middle of the "LONELY HEARTS" on the drumhead, it bisects into the phrase "I ONE IX HE DIE," which some have read as "November 9, He Die."

6 The *cor anglais* that McCartney is holding is black (symbolizing death) and wooden (coffin).

> " **I AM ALIVE AND WELL AND UNCONCERNED ABOUT THE RUMORS OF MY DEATH. BUT IF I WERE DEAD, I WOULD BE THE LAST TO KNOW." ** Paul McCartney, 1969

ABOVE RIGHT: A "collector's edition" fan magazine published in 1969 at the height of the "Paul is Dead" furor.

BELOW RIGHT: A member of the Ontario Provincial Police, with "O.P.D." badge on his shoulder, on parade in 1967.

7 The Japanese doll at the feet of the wax figure Beatles has a line on its head, representing the wounds Paul sustained in the crash.

8 The Indian Shiva doll is a symbol of destruction and creation, and one of its four arms points at the wax Paul, while another points at Paul himself.

9 On the back cover, Paul has his back to the camera, revealing three black buttons on his coat, which represent the mourning of the other Beatles. He also appears taller, suggesting that he is ascending. Next to his head is the lyric "WITHOUT YOU."

10 Also on the back cover, George's hand points at a lyric from "She's Leaving Home," "Wednesday morning at five o'clock"—supposedly indicating the time of Paul's crash.

THE LOOK

Two weeks later, on June 1, *Sgt. Pepper* was released in the UK to ecstatic reviews (the album's US release followed a day later).

While most concentrated on the music and the Beatles' ability to tap into the cultural moment (Kenneth Tynan, a critic for the London *Times*, famously describing it as "a decisive moment in the history of Western civilization"), a few reviews of the album mentioned the cover—but not always in a favorable light. The *New York Times* called it "busy, hip, and cluttered," while *Record Mirror* griped, "The packaging, while fairly inventive and lavish, is not as attractive as it might be."

Nevertheless, fans were entranced. Typical were the reactions of subscribers to *The Beatles Monthly Book* magazine, which included:

"Cover worth every penny spent on designing it."
"FANTABULASTICOUS!!"
"Thank you for the words, the big middle picture and of course, the cutouts!"

Aside from its engaging visuals, the cover was the first gatefold, and the first with song lyrics printed in full. The Beatles' publisher, Northern Songs, objected to the latter, thinking it would undermine sheet music sales (still a viable means of income in 1967). There was also to be a "packet of goodies" (an envelope including candy and decals) inside the sleeve, but as Blake has said, "It wasn't practical. So there was the compromise of a flat packet which slid in easily."

The cutouts—badges, stripes, and mustache—had the feel of a cereal-box

fan-club prize, and were presented in a collage by Blake and Haworth (the original version of which was auctioned in 2012 for £88,000). Finally, the album's inner sleeve featured artwork by The Fool (alas, Fraser couldn't block them completely), which replaced the standard white paper with an abstract

STEREO

pattern of red and white—another first for an LP release.

The final cost for the artwork was nearly £3,000—an extravagant sum for a time when album covers typically cost around £75. Copyright and retouching fees for the crowd came to £1,367. Robert Fraser and Michael Cooper's fees were £1,500, out of which Peter Blake and Jann Haworth received £200. EMI honcho Joe Lockwood later told Robert Fraser he could've hired the whole London Symphony Orchestra for what the cover cost. John Lennon said, "It was the most expensive album, and of course, the record company was screaming at the price of the cover. And now it's probably pinned all over walls."

Blake and Haworth won the 1968 Grammy Award for Best Album Cover (one of four trophies the album received that year; the others were for Best Contemporary Album, Best Engineered Recording, and Album of the Year). And if imitation is the sincerest form of flattery, then no cover has enjoyed as much. It's been parodied by *MAD Magazine*, the Rutles, Frank Zappa & the Mothers of Invention, *Sesame Street*, *The Simpsons*, and hundreds of others. Even the artists have created their own updated versions—Blake with a selection of contemporary heroes (Helen Mirren, David Bowie), Haworth with a more racially and sexually integrated crowd, displayed as public art in Salt Lake City.

Sgt. Pepper remains the Mona Lisa of album covers, an iconic image that is recognized the world over. And, like that great work, it engages us through both what it does and doesn't reveal. It invites repeated inspection and questions. It teases with mysteries. It strikes a posture of celebration and challenge. And, by juxtaposing great intellectuals with pop figures, it breaks down notions of high and low, and in doing so reflects the eclectic styles of the songs, from music hall to rock 'n' roll to Indian.

Most of all, it places the Beatles rightly in a context of twentieth-century art and culture, elevating them, as they'd hoped,

beyond mop-tops to artists. They're not so much standing on the shoulders of giants as standing shoulder-to-shoulder with them.

"It combines the past and the then contemporary, the exotic and the banal—it's a hybrid," says Haworth, who at seventy-three is still creating, teaching, and exhibiting, often in collaboration with her children.

"The piece taken as a whole really is like a movie," she adds, "in that it's a combo of cameraman, designers, costumers, musicians, lighting, direction, and acting a part. Yet, for all that is said about it, I still do not consider it very important. It's really the

ABOVE LEFT: "SLC Pepper," one of several remakes of the Beatles' LP cover produced by Jann Haworth.

ABOVE RIGHT: A US newspaper rack advertising a six-part series on "the new Beatles."

OPPOSITE, LEFT: Haworth today, standing in front of an outtake from the *Sgt. Pepper* shoot.

OPPOSITE, RIGHT: Peter Blake with a framed copy of what remains his most famous work.

music that's the main event. As for the cover, it is only a record cover. It is not the Salk vaccine or the Hubble Space Telescope.

"Also, in hindsight, it's sad to realize how many people around the project died young—John, George, Mal, Brian, Michael, Michael's wife. A very high price was paid for flying so high."

Though Peter Blake, now eighty-three, went on to create many well-known rock covers, such as the Who's *Face Dances* and the "Do They Know It's Christmas?" single and still exhibits, he's had an uneasy relationship with *Pepper*, mostly because of the retouching that was done without his or Haworth's approval.

"The sky, the palm tree—it was not done very sympathetically," he later said. "I was very unhappy with it. The cover was meant to be a happening, an environment, but all that got lost. Retouching killed the idea of it being three-dimensional. Looking back, it would have been much easier to have just made a collage. I could have done it in a couple of days."

Fifty years on, the surviving Beatles have no hesitation in praising the cover. Ringo said, "*Sgt. Pepper* was a special album, so when the time came for the sleeve we wanted to dress up, and we wanted to be these people. . . . It was flower power coming into the fullest.

It was love and peace. It was a fabulous period, for me and the world."

"The album was a big production, and we wanted the album sleeve to be really interesting," McCartney said, looking back on its creation for *The Beatles Anthology*. "We realized for the first time that some day someone would actually be holding a thing they'd call 'The Beatles new LP' and that normally it would just be a collection of songs or a nice picture on the cover, nothing more. So the idea was to do a complete thing that you could make what you liked of: a magic presentation . . . It took a lot of working out, but it's one of the all-time [greatest] covers, so that was great."

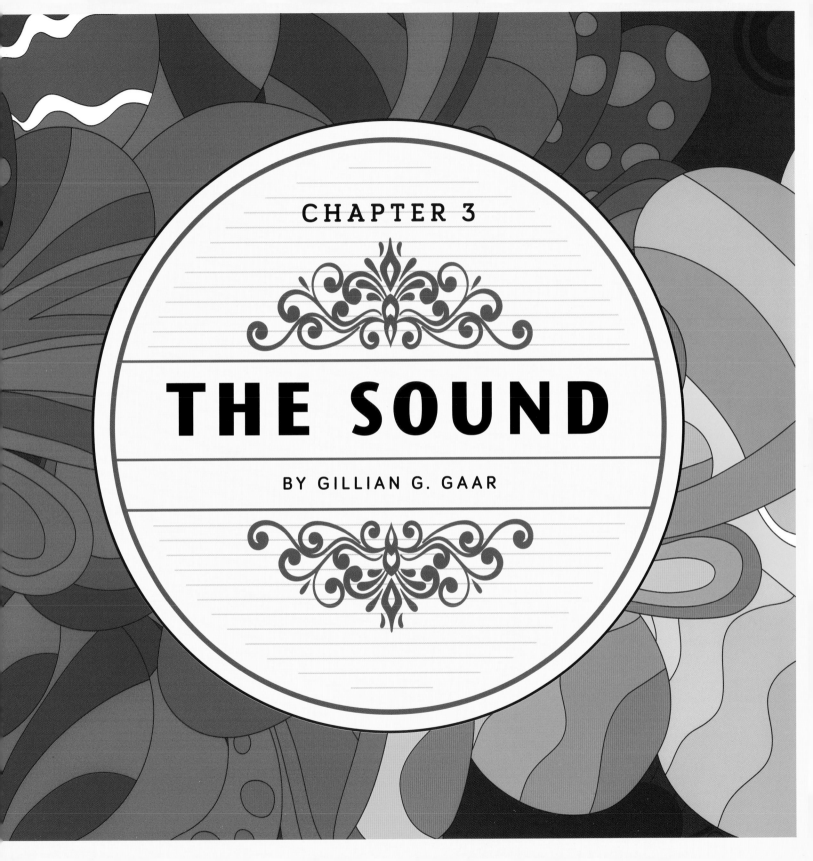

CHAPTER 3

THE SOUND

BY GILLIAN G. GAAR

> "You just have to keep striving for perfection. This LP, I think, is the best we've done, but only the best we could do at that time. The next one ought to be better."
>
> George Harrison to the *NME*, 1967

FIFTY MONTHS. That's the span of time between the Beatles' recording session for their first single, "Love Me Do," in September 1962 and the first session for the *Sgt. Pepper* album in November 1966. It was an extraordinary period of artistic growth for a band to make in just over four years, an arc surpassing the achievements of every other rock act of the era, with the possible exception of the Beach Boys. But though no one realized it at the time, Brian Wilson, the Beach Boys' primary songwriter, had peaked in 1966 with *Pet Sounds* and "Good Vibrations," high-water marks from which there was nowhere for him to go but down. In contrast, the Beatles were to continue their ascent, working assiduously over a period of five months to bring what would be the most glittering creation of their careers to life.

On November 24, 1966, the four Beatles reconvened at what was then still called EMI Recording Studios. (The studio wouldn't take on the name Abbey Road Studios until the Beatles made the location iconic with the release of their *Abbey Road* album.) It was their first recording session in over five months. The previous summer had been an exceptionally fraught time for the band, with their final world tour plagued with difficulties. In Japan, they received death threats from right-wing nationalists offended that a rock group was scheduled to play at the Nippon Budokan hall, generally reserved for martial arts exhibitions; in the Philippines, security was withdrawn when they inadvertently missed a reception that first lady Imelda Marcos had planned for them, resulting in much bad feeling and culminating in them being punched and spat on as they made their way through the airport. And John Lennon's quote in an interview he did with Maureen Cleave for the *Evening Standard* in March 1966, asserting that the Beatles were "more popular than Jesus" led to controversy—and more death threats—in the United States.

Small wonder, then, that following the Beatles' last concert in San Francisco on August 29, 1966, as their plane spirited them back to Los Angeles, George Harrison announced, "Well, that's it. I'm not a Beatle anymore" as he sank into his seat. Touring had become a joyless grind. The concerts gave audiences no clue as to the musical development the Beatles had been making in the studio; the 1966 tour marked the first time in the band's history that they didn't play a single song from their most recent album (*Revolver*). With the band hampered by their inability to showcase their new material in concert properly, and feeling that their musicianship as live players was deteriorating, touring no longer brought any satisfaction.

BEATLES, GO HOME!

That was the chant as an airport crowd jostled and jeered the boys in 'snub' row

THEY TREATED US LIKE ANIMALS, SAYS RINGO

PREVIOUS SPREAD: John Lennon, Ringo Starr, and Paul McCartney play pianos at EMI Studios.

ABOVE: A *Daily Mirror* report on unrest during the Beatles' trip to the Philippines in July 1966.

RIGHT: Teenagers gather at a "Beatles Burning" in Georgia in response to John Lennon's claim that the band is "more popular than Jesus."

FAR RIGHT: Concert tickets and a tour program from the band's shows in Japan in July 1966.

Following the tour, each band member took an extended break from being "The Beatles." Lennon signed on for a small role in the anti-war film *How I Won the War*, directed by Richard Lester (who had previously directed the Fab Four in *A Hard Day's Night* and *Help!*). Harrison spent over a month in India, studying sitar with Ravi Shankar. Paul McCartney began writing music for the film *The Family Way* and took an extended road trip through France and Africa. Ringo Starr hung out at home with his wife and child, and visited Lennon when filming for *How I Won the War* moved to Spain. The lack of any professional public appearances led to news stories that the Beatles were on the verge of breaking up. The Beatles denied they

had any such plans. But they did realize that they were at a crossroads.

And when they came together again—when they had to pick up the mantle of being "The Beatles" again— they were determined to exercise a greater control over their career. Though the band had returned to the studio, EMI knew there was no chance of getting a new Beatles album out in time for the lucrative Christmas market. Beatles producer George Martin had already been remixing songs for a "best-of" set with the unimaginative title *A Collection of Beatles Oldies* (with the additional tag . . . *But Goldies!* on the back cover), released in December in the UK to plug the gap. But it was still hoped that the group might at least be able to

come up with a pre-holiday single; after all, they'd managed to complete the "Paperback Writer" / "Rain" single, released earlier in the year, in two days.

But the Beatles were now calling the shots, and they were in no mood to be rushed. They had no interest in adhering to anyone's timetable. Since EMI owned the venue, there was no limit placed on their time in the studio, or what hours they would keep; typically, sessions began in the evening and went on until the early hours of the morning.

A further restraint was removed by their decision to stop touring; they no longer had to be concerned about whether they'd be able to perform their new songs in concert. In their most recent recordings, the Beatles had been

> **WITH ANY KIND OF THING, MY AIM SEEMS TO BE TO DISTORT IT. DISTORT IT FROM WHAT WE KNOW IT AS, EVEN WITH MUSIC, WITH VISUAL THINGS. BUT THE AIM IS TO CHANGE IT FROM WHAT IT IS TO SEE WHAT IT COULD BE." Paul McCartney, 1966

increasingly delving into sonic experimentation, effectively using the studio as an instrument in its own right. The fadeout of "Rain" has the song playing backward, and *Revolver* not only utilized that trick, but several others as well. The album's last track, "Tomorrow Never Knows," was inspired in part by *Gesang der Jünglinge* by the German composer and electronic music pioneer Karlheinz Stockhausen, a landmark work that blends the human voice with electronically generated sounds and was later hailed as "the first masterpiece of electronic music." For "Tomorrow Never Knows," the Beatles made use of backward tapes; loops of sounds that float in and out of the mix; vocals and instruments put through a

revolving Leslie speaker, giving them an additional fuzziness; and something they would draw on heavily for *Sgt. Pepper*: automatic double-tracking, or ADT (also referred to as artificial double-tracking).

ADT was created as a timesaving device by Ken Townsend, one of EMI's sound engineers. The Beatles, especially Lennon, had tired of double-tracking— having to sing the same part twice. With ADT, double-tracking could be created by the use of tape delay; it took the vocal and sent it to a second tape machine, allowing it to be delayed in the final mix.

"If you think in photographic terms, it's like having two negatives," Martin explained in the *Beatles Anthology*. "When you get one negative exactly on

top of the other, there's just one picture. So if you have one sound image on top of the other exactly, then it becomes only one image. But move it slightly, by a few milliseconds, and around eight or nine milliseconds it gives you a boxy telephone-like quality."

In trying to explain the process to Lennon, Martin jokingly told him his voice was being treated with a "double-bifurcated sploshing flange," resulting in Lennon forever referring to ADT as "flanging." The term stuck, and is still used today; to Martin's amusement, he later asked an American engineer where the term had come from and was told, "It's an effect you can get by pushing your thumb on the flange of the tape reel."

Phasing was similar to ADT in the sense of being another way of adding delay to a vocal or instrument. The Beatles would also make great use of varispeeding—altering the pitch of a recording—beginning with the first track they recorded in November, "Strawberry Fields Forever." Echo was routinely applied to vocals and instruments, while engineer Geoff Emerick devised new ways of recording the band, building on the work of the previous engineer who worked with the group, Norman Smith. He placed more microphones around Starr's drum kit, and moved the mics closer to the drums. He put screens around the guitar amplifiers (something Smith had not done), isolating the sound. McCartney was now recording his bass parts on a separate track (where previously they'd often been recorded on the same track as the drums), something he credited with allowing him to develop more melodic bass lines. Emerick further played with the bass sound by placing microphones at two different distances from McCartney's bass amp, and mixing the two signals together. The bass signal could also be boosted by plugging the instrument directly into the mixing console via a DIT (Direct Injection Transformer) box, another of Townsend's creations.

The Beatles' initial guitar/bass/drums setup was now merely a foundation upon which the group laid innumerable overdubs and an increasingly varied amount of instruments. Their boundless creativity could no longer be contained by the antiquated four-track recording setup at EMI's studios (where eight-track recording would not be available until May 1968). Instead, the group relied upon reduction mixes; once the four tracks of a tape were full, they would be mixed down to one or two tracks, then bounced down to another machine, thus freeing up additional tracks for overdubs. During the *Sgt. Pepper* era, two or even three reduction mixes would be made. Some sound quality was lost during the process, but it was felt the advantage of having more tracks to play with was more than enough compensation.

The Beatles worked on three songs in December 1966: "Strawberry Fields Forever," "Penny Lane," and "When I'm Sixty-Four." The first two were soon commandeered for a single (released in February 1967) and marked a natural progression of the types of aural experimentation heard on *Revolver*, "Tomorrow Never Knows" in particular. In comparison, "When I'm Sixty-Four" was relatively straightforward. But it was nonetheless as different in its own way to the kind of music the Beatles had previously released.

McCartney had written the song when he was sixteen, "thinking it could come in handy in a musical comedy or something"; the Beatles had even played an early version of it during their club days when their amplifiers broke down, as a way of amusing the audience until repairs could be made. Now it had evolved into a vaudevillian pastiche, perfectly reflecting the current vogue in London for kitschy Victoriana, peddled by such self-consciously named shops as I Was Lord Kitchner's Valet.

The Beatles began work on the track on December 6. The musical backing was suitably genteel; McCartney played bass and piano, Lennon played guitar, and Starr played drums and chimes. McCartney, Lennon, and Harrison provided backing vocals (Harrison's only contribution to the track). The song's music-hall quotient was further enhanced by the addition of two B-flat clarinets and a bass clarinet. McCartney's lead vocal underscored the whimsy: it was sped up, raising the pitch by a

The Beatles and George Martin (*center*) take a tea break during the *Pepper* sessions, March 30, 1967.

semitone, and made him sound more youthful, though in his recollection he did it to emphasize the tongue-in-cheek nature of the song.

But though McCartney exudes his usual cheerfulness during the number, there's certainly discord in the song's lyric, which expresses a fear of abandonment, with the narrator essentially asking, "Will you still want me when I'm old and gray?"

The perennially sunny optimism in McCartney's delivery indicates that a happy ending will result in the end. But it is indicative of a sense of unease that would permeate a number of tracks on the upcoming album, its largely upbeat reputation notwithstanding.

In January 1967, the decision was made to not only release "Penny Lane" and "Strawberry Fields Forever" as a single but also to not include them on

The Liverpool Songs

T HE FIRST SONGS released from the *Sgt. Pepper* sessions were "Strawberry Fields Forever" and "Penny Lane," the only Beatles songs to reference specific Liverpool sites.

"Strawberry Fields Forever" was written in the fall of 1966, when Lennon was filming *How I Won the War* in Almeria, Spain. The name came from a Salvation Army-run children's home in his neighborhood, though it was called Strawberry Field, singular. Lennon and his friends attended garden parties at Strawberry Field; at other times they'd sneak in, climbing the wall around the property, to play in the extensive grounds.

Lennon talked at length about the song's meaning in the last major interview of his life, with *Playboy* magazine. "I just took the name—it had nothing to do with the Salvation Army," he said. "As an image—Strawberry Fields for ever." But Lennon's look back at his childhood was filled with unease, as he elliptically referred to the isolation he felt as a child. "What I'm saying, in my insecure way, is, nobody seems to understand where I'm coming from.

I seem to see things in a different way from most people." He'd expressed his feelings of insecurity before, as in "I'm a Loser" and "Help!," but never quite so poetically as he does here.

When Lennon first played the song for George Martin on November 24, 1966, accompanying himself on acoustic guitar, it made an immediate impression. "It was completely unlike anything we had done before," Martin said. "It was dreamlike without being fey, weird without being pretentious."

The band immediately set to work on the song, and the first version does have a delicacy that had not been present in any previous Beatles song. Aside from Lennon's languid vocal, the most distinctive sound is that of the Mellotron, played by Paul McCartney. The Mellotron was an early type of a synthesizer, a keyboard that used tapes that could be programmed to emulate different sounds; for "Strawberry Fields Forever"

it was set to sound like a flute. The other unusual part is a slide guitar line, played by George Harrison. Lennon's vocal was double-tracked, with McCartney and Harrison providing backing vocals. The song was finished—or so they thought.

Lennon wasn't entirely happy with how the song sounded, so on November 28 and 29, the band recorded a new version. This version is far less pastoral; the slide guitar was gone, though the Mellotron was recognized as being integral to the sound, and Lennon's lead vocal was given ADT and sped up. The lyrics had also been amended, now opening with the chorus—"Let me take you down"—a more welcoming invitation to the listener.

But Lennon still wasn't happy, and on December 8, work began on another, more elaborate arrangement, with the guitar-bass-drums lineup embellished by timpani and other percussive instruments. Starr's cymbals were

THE BEATLES

ABOVE LEFT: John Lennon's lyrics to "Strawberry Fields Forever," as written on a sheet of Lufthansa headed notepaper.

ABOVE RIGHT: A reissue of "Strawberry Fields Forever" / "Penny Lane," as included in *The Singles Collection 1962–1970,* a twenty-two-disc set of seven-inch singles released in 1976.

recorded and played backward, and Martin wrote a score for four trumpets and three cellos. The most exotic touch came from Harrison, who played the swarmandal. Lennon's vocals were again sped up.

Now Lennon gave his producer a new challenge. He liked the dreaminess of the version they'd recorded in late November, but also the wild feeling of the more recent version. Could they be combined? Martin, working with Geoff Emerick, realized that by speeding up the earlier version and slowing down the latter, the two different recordings could

be brought into the same tempo and the same key. A coda was also added. By 3:30, the music has faded away, only to reemerge a few seconds later, the band jamming away, and Lennon's ghostly voice heard solemnly, if inexplicably, intoning, "Cranberry sauce."

Lennon's drawing on his Liverpool roots prompted McCartney to do the same with "Penny Lane," named for a Liverpool street, with the song's narrative eye particularly focused on the Penny Lane roundabout.

"Penny Lane was a place with a lot of character and a lot of characters,"

THE SOUND

103

McCartney later observed. "Good material for writing." As clean and precise as "Strawberry Fields" was languorous and gauzy, "Penny Lane" drew quick portraits of the area's quirky residents—the barber, the banker, the fireman—and, in McCartney's words, "arted it up a little bit," giving the song a surreal veneer.

Work began on December 29. Piano is the dominant sound throughout the track, with several piano parts recorded; one was played through a Vox guitar amplifier, with reverb added; another was played at half-speed and then sped up on replay. A whistle effect from a harmonium was fed through the Vox guitar amp. McCartney's lead vocal, and Lennon's backing vocal, were recorded at a slow speed to sound sped-up on replay. Guitar, bass, and drums were also recorded at a slower speed and

heavily limited (taking off the top end). Various percussion instruments were used, including a hand bell.

Martin's skills as an arranger were again drawn on to provide a score for the four flutes, two oboes, two English horns, two trumpets, two piccolos, flugelhorn, and double-bass to play. The finishing touch came when McCartney tuned in to the BBC2 TV program *Masterworks* on January 11, 1967, and heard the English Chamber Orchestra playing Bach's Brandenburg Concerto No. 2 in F Major, with David Mason on piccolo trumpet. Mason was duly hired to play the instrument on "Penny Lane," McCartney singing the part while Martin wrote it down. A final trumpet passage from Mason appeared on the US promo single, but was cut from the official release.

It was first considered that "Strawberry

> **STRAWBERRY FIELDS IS A REAL PLACE. AFTER I STOPPED LIVING AT PENNY LANE, I MOVED IN WITH MY AUNTIE WHO LIVED IN THE SUBURBS IN A NICE SEMIDETACHED PLACE WITH A SMALL GARDEN AND DOCTORS AND LAWYERS AND THAT ILK LIVING AROUND . . . NOT THE POOR SLUMMY KIND OF IMAGE THAT WAS PROJECTED IN ALL THE BEATLES STORIES."** John Lennon, 1980

Fields" be paired with "When I'm Sixty-Four" for single release, until it was then decided that "Penny Lane" would be the stronger song. The single was released February 13, 1967, in the US, and February 17 in the UK, as a double A-side single. In the US, "Penny

Lane" placed higher, topping the charts in *Billboard*, *Cash Box*, and *Record World* ("Strawberry Fields" placed No. 8, No. 10, and No. 9, respectively). But in the UK, the single stalled at No. 2 on most charts, kept at bay by Engelbert Humperdinck's "Release Me." It was the first Beatles single that failed to top the charts since "From Me to You" (though it nonetheless topped *Melody Maker*'s chart, staying at no. 1 for three weeks), prompting a spate of "Are the Beatles finished?" headlines.

Just as flummoxing to some were the promotional films the band made for the songs, which were shot on January 30, 31, and February 7, at Knole Park in Sevenoaks, Kent, and on February 5 at Angel Lane, Stratford, East London. When the clips were screened on the US show *American Bandstand*, many of the comments from the studio audience reflected a confusion:

"They looked older and it ruins their image."

"Their mustaches are weird."

"It reminded me of Hollywood about a hundred years ago."

Adding to the atmosphere of surrealism in the promo films, the Beatles weren't seen miming—still a rarity in videos today.

The single nonetheless heightened anticipation for *Sgt. Pepper*, which wouldn't be released for another four months. Unabashedly English, the songs also displayed the Beatles' penchant for giving the seemingly commonplace an unexpected twist.

As McCartney later put it: "We always liked to take those ordinary facts of northern working-class life . . . and mystify them and glamorize them and make them into something more magical, more universal."

RIGHT: The gates to the real Strawberry Field, a Salvation Army Children's Home in Woolton, Liverpool.

" THE ONLY REASON THAT 'STRAWBERRY FIELDS FOREVER' AND 'PENNY LANE' DIDN'T GO ONTO THE NEW ALBUM WAS A FEELING THAT IF WE ISSUED A SINGLE, IT SHOULDN'T GO ONTO AN ALBUM. IT'S NONSENSE THESE DAYS, BUT IN THOSE DAYS . . . WE'D TRY TO GIVE THE PUBLIC VALUE FOR MONEY." George Martin

the subsequent album. Their release on a single didn't necessarily preclude that from happening; of the seven UK albums the Beatles had released at that point, four had contained tracks that had also been released as singles (indeed, their debut album, *Please Please Me*, was named after a single). But in this case, the single would not be included on the album, leaving the door open for never-ending speculation as to what songs might have been left off *Sgt. Pepper* if this had not been the case (presumably the songs recorded at the end of the sessions).

There was also another number recorded in January that would not be included on the album. On January 5, following some overdubbing work on "Penny Lane," the Beatles recorded an improvisational piece for an upcoming multimedia event to be held at the Roundhouse in North London on January 28 and February 4. The event was variously called the Million Volt Light and Sound Rave and the Carnival of Light, hence the track itself being referred to as "Carnival of Light." Aside from its airings at the Roundhouse events, the track has never been released, or even escaped on a bootleg. Beatles historian Mark Lewisohn

described the thirteen minute and forty-eight second piece as featuring distorted guitars, organ, and drums, various sound effects drenched in "heaps" of tape echo, "manic" tambourine, and Lennon and McCartney's voices "screaming dementedly and bawling aloud random phrases like 'Are you all right?' and 'Barcelona!'" Though the Beatles, especially McCartney, had been investigating London's burgeoning countercultural arts scene, this was their first direct—albeit anonymous—participation in that scene. And that freewheeling spirit of improvisation would have a decided impact on the next track the band would work on.

I'D LOVE TO TURN YOU ON
"A Day in the Life" is the Beatles' magnum opus, regularly cited as the most important song the band ever recorded. In his efforts to come up with songs for the new album, Lennon drew inspiration from the newspaper, specifically citing a *Daily Mail* story about the death of Tara Browne, heir to the Guinness fortune, and a friend to the Beatles, who'd died in a car crash in London on December 16, 1966. Browne was referenced as the man who "blew

his mind out in a car," though McCartney later said he wasn't aware of the connection: "I was imagining a politician bombed out on drugs."

For the song's second verse, Lennon alluded to his recent work on *How I Won the War*. Then, stuck, he sought McCartney's help in completing it.

Lennon would later note his partner's initial reluctance to contribute. "He was a bit shy about it, 'cause I think he thought, 'Well, it's a good song,'" he told *Playboy*. "Sometimes we wouldn't let each other interfere with a song . . . 'cause you tend to be a bit lax with somebody else's stuff—you experiment a bit." But McCartney had a scrap of a song describing the morning routine of heading off to school that Lennon agreed would fit. Another *Daily Mail* story about the number of potholes in Blackburn, Lancashire, provided further inspiration, McCartney enjoying the way Lennon pronounced the word as people would in northern England: "Lan-ca-sheer."

Then McCartney came up with the line "I'd love to turn you on," at which point the two looked at each other, feeling the same frisson of excitement as when they'd added the words "turn me on" to "She's a Woman." Did they

The handwritten draft reads:

I read the news today, oh boy
about a lucky man who made the grade
and though the news was rather sad
well I just had to laugh
I saw the photograph
He blew his mind out in a car
he didn't notice that the lights had changed
a crowd of people stood and stared
they'd seen his face before
though they didn't know if he was really from
the house of lords.
I saw a film today, oh boy
The English Army had just won the war
a crowd of people turned away
well I just had to look
having read the book.
I read the news today, oh boy
4000 holes in Blackburn Lancashire
and they I the holes were very small
They had to count them all
now they knew how many holes it takes to fill
the Albert Hall

ABOVE: The crushed wreckage of Tara Browne's Lotus Elan, following his fatal crash in Kensington, London, December 18, 1966.

ABOVE RIGHT: John Lennon's first draft of "A Day in the Life," as sold at auction in 2006.

dare make such a direct reference to taking drugs? They decided they did, reasoning that the phrase had other meanings as well. But McCartney now felt the song needed "something amazing" to fully flesh it out.

The first session for "A Day in the Life" was held on January 19. (As work on *Sgt. Pepper* gathered steam, the Beatles rarely worked straight through on a track; they routinely stopped work on one song to begin work on another, then later returned to working on the earlier track.) Thanks to the many bootlegs in circulation, it's possible to hear this monumental track in various stages of development. As Martin observed, the initial, unadorned takes (featuring only guitar, piano, bongos, and maracas) are "so charming, so natural." It has the same simplicity as the early takes of "Strawberry Fields."

The Beatles knew they wanted something to fill the transition between Lennon's verses and McCartney's vignette; on the early takes, Beatles roadie Mal Evans can be heard counting out the bars, his voice increasingly echo-laden as he continues, and setting off an alarm clock when reaching twenty-four. He can still be heard counting in the final version of the song.

It was McCartney who came up with the idea that would make the song take an inspired leap into the avant-garde. As the sole Beatle living in London, he'd been the one most likely to be seen at gallery openings, experimental music

> **"IT WAS ABOUT ME REMEMBERING WHAT IT WAS LIKE TO RUN UP THE ROAD TO CATCH THE BUS TO SCHOOL, HAVING A SMOKE AND GOING INTO SCHOOL. . . . THAT WAS THE ONLY SONG ON THE ALBUM WRITTEN AS A DELIBERATE PROVOCATION."** Paul McCartney on "A Day in the Life"

concerts, and other "happenings" of the era. Barry Miles, cofounder of London's Indica Bookshop and Gallery, and the author of McCartney's official biography, *Many Years from Now*, writes that in the two years prior to *Pepper*, McCartney was "at his most inquisitive and receptive, listening to every type of music, going to art openings and attending experimental plays." Instead of working with tape loops, as they had on *Revolver*, McCartney wanted to draw on the power of a symphony orchestra to create some kind of "freak out"— "a sound building up from nothing to the end of the world," as Lennon later put it to their producer.

Martin resisted the great financial extravagance of utilizing a full orchestra of ninety players but agreed to assemble a smaller group of forty. The Beatles decided to make the orchestral session, held on February 10, an event—a "happening"—and asked the musicians to wear evening dress. The band members themselves sported the latest in Swinging London finery, brought along bagfuls of funny props (party hats, balloons, fake noses and glasses, a fake gorilla's paw), and invited a number of their musician friends—including Mick Jagger and Marianne Faithfull,

Donovan, Mike Nesmith, and Graham Nash, among others—to join the fun. Film cameras were also present to capture the action for a proposed television special (an idea that was ultimately scrapped).

To accommodate everyone, the session was held in Abbey Road's largest room, Studio One. McCartney's brief was a simple one: each musician was to go from the lowest note they could play on their instrument to the highest, taking care to not play in unison, over the course of twenty-four bars. But Martin knew the trained symphony men would need a bit more instruction, so he wrote out a modified score to keep the rise from being entirely random. Everyone would start on their low note and hold it for eight bars, taking off on the ninth, with the score marking where in the rise the player should be at a particular bar. The musicians would end on an E-major chord. If not quite the wild improv of McCartney's dreams, it was still unstructured enough to bemuse the musicians, who nonetheless entered into the spirit of things by donning the fake glasses and noses.

With McCartney and Martin conducting, the orchestral ascent was recorded five times: once on the mix-

down tape that had the Beatles' rhythm backing and vocals, and four more times on a second tape, filling all four tracks (meaning you're hearing equivalent of two hundred musicians). There was a problem in syncing the two tapes together, as they had to be manually started at the same time; a careful listen reveals that the orchestra goes in and out of time.

The ascent was used in two places: between Lennon and McCartney's verses, and then again after Lennon's final verse. But how to end the song after that final impressive chord? The first idea was to record a number of people humming a sustained note— something that was attempted after the orchestral recording was finished. On February 22, a new approach was taken, with Lennon, McCartney, Starr, and Evans recorded each playing an E-major chord on different pianos (with Martin also playing harmonium), holding the delay pedals so the chords were sustained; as they played, Geoff Emerick slowly raised the volume faders to capture every bit of sound as it faded away. It took nine takes to capture just the right sound. Afterward, the group blew off steam by recording an improvisational piece, described by

ABOVE LEFT: Paul
McCartney conducts the
orchestra during a
session for "A Day in the
Life," February 10, 1967.

ABOVE RIGHT: The
Beatles—and some of
the friends they invited
along to the studio for
the day—listen to a
playback of "A Day in
the Life."

FOLLOWING SPREAD:
Another shot of the
orchestral session for
"A Day in the Life."

Mark Lewisohn as "22 minutes, 10 seconds of drum beat, augmented by tambourine and congas. Quite what it was meant for is not clear." The piece has never been released.

Like the final version of "Strawberry Fields," "A Day in the Life" begins quietly, in a manner not too dissimilar to its early takes, with its gently strummed guitar, restrained piano, and maracas. It features one of Lennon's most evocative vocals. Never had he sounded so world-weary, the double-tracking making his voice even more resonant. Starr's drums come in on the second verse, the tom-toms thundering like timpani, after Emerick suggested that Starr tune them so low their skins went slack; Emerick also removed the bottom skins on the tom-toms and miked the drums from underneath.

The orchestra finally comes in as the last notes of Lennon's "turn you on" fade away, the music swirling in anticipation before the musicians begin their liftoff. Fortuitously, the alarm clock that goes off before McCartney starts singing neatly cues his opening line: "Woke up." Wanting it to sound like McCartney really had just woken up, Emerick removed the treble from his vocal and compressed it, in order to make it sound "muzzy." And McCartney's snapshot of everyday life takes its own surreal turn as the narrator slips into a dream and the orchestra returns, playing a series of block chords. Lennon's laconic non sequitur about the holes in the streets of Blackburn filling the Albert Hall is nicely juxtaposed with the final moment of transcendence, when the orchestra makes its second ascent, ending in triumph before the final piano chord slams in with a weighty gravitas.

LEFT: Paul McCartney and Mal Evans return to London following a week-long trip to Denver and San Francisco, April 12, 1967.

> **SUDDENLY ON THE PLANE I GOT THIS IDEA. I THOUGHT, 'LET'S NOT BE OURSELVES. LET'S DEVELOP ALTER EGOS SO WE'RE NOT HAVING TO PROJECT AN IMAGE WHICH WE KNOW. IT WOULD BE MUCH MORE FREE.'"** Paul McCartney, 1994

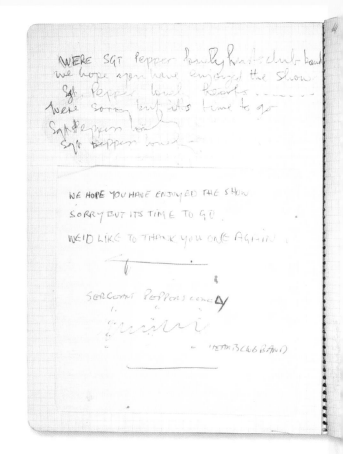

RIGHT: An early draft of Paul McCartney's lyrics to "Sgt. Pepper's Lonely Hearts Club Band," as written in a notebook belonging to Mal Evans.

It remains the most stunning song in the Beatles' catalog.

INTRODUCING THE BAND

The album finally took on a theme on February 1, when the band began work on what would become the title track: "Sgt. Pepper's Lonely Hearts Club Band." There are varying accounts as to where the concept came from and how much it really influenced the making of the album. McCartney has said the idea of creating an alter ego for the Beatles came to him as he flew home from his trip to France and Africa the previous year. He'd briefly traveled in disguise earlier on his trip and was now excited by the idea of creating another identity for the band. "We could say, 'How would somebody else sing this? He might approach it a bit more sarcastically, perhaps' . . . then when John came up to the microphone or I did, it wouldn't be John or Paul singing, it would be the members of this band. It would be a freeing element." "Sgt. Pepper" was a play on the salt and pepper packets provided with the meal served on that plane flight back from Africa (both McCartney and Mal Evans have been variously credited with thinking it up). The full name, "Sgt. Pepper's Lonely Hearts Club Band," referenced the current penchant for whimsical band names, like the Strawberry Alarm Clock, the Chocolate Watchband, Lothar and the Hand People, and Dr. West's Medicine Show and Junk Band.

Yet McCartney didn't mention his idea when the Beatles began recording back in November 1966, and it hadn't played a role in any of the songs they'd recorded so far; clearly, Lennon wasn't singing "A Day in the Life" as "somebody else." George Martin has said that the "concept" idea wasn't mentioned by McCartney until after the song "Sgt. Pepper" was recorded. And while McCartney has insisted, "Everyone was into it," the other Beatles seem to have merely gone along with the idea without the same level of enthusiasm. "All my contributions to the album have absolutely nothing to do with this idea

The Magic Piano

By Dudley Edwards

> **"I** WROTE 'GETTING BETTER,' 'Sgt. Pepper's Lonely Hearts Club Band,' and 'Fixing a Hole' on my magic piano; of course the way in which it was painted added to the fun of it all. I still cherish jealously my piano, on which I also composed 'Hey Jude.' It's in its rightful place in my music room in London." Paul McCartney

Douglas Binder and I began designing Paul's "Magic Piano" in September '66 and completed it in October of that year. When it came to choosing motifs and designs, we wanted something that exuded joy, and when I considered what kind of imagery epitomized that for me, I was taken back to my early days of rock 'n' roll, with Teddy Boys bopping and jiving to Little Richard around a fairground Waltzer. I figured an intrinsic part of that package was fairground imagery; this was a form of folk art worth proliferating, but in a new way.

Our designs comprised a synthesis of the following: a love of basic geometry, elements of Art Deco, primitive folk art, and sophisticated color combinations. At that time we chose a look that was smooth and polished (almost mechanical), with hard-edge lines and smooth gradation. This required the painterly skills that Doug and I learned at art college, where in those days part of the curriculum involved the acquisition of heraldry and coach-painting techniques.

I believe these early formative experiences of creating a synthesis of fairground art and rock 'n' roll were something that we shared with both the Beatles and Peter Blake. Its applications are evident not only in the piano but in the *Sgt. Pepper* album cover and certain tracks like "For the Benefit of Mr. Kite!"

When Douglas and I went our separate ways, Paul invited me to come and live with him while I painted a mural for the interior of his house. I recollect that when I first arrived at Paul's I had to run the gauntlet of screaming girls who seemed to congregate outside on a permanent basis. Paul couldn't have been more welcoming or more generous; when I mentioned that I only had the clothes I was wearing, he opened his wardrobe and said, "Help yourself."

Paul included me in all his social and business activities, so it became difficult to find time for working on the mural. As he was the only Beatle based in central London at the time, his house had many cultural visitors. I recall evenings with Mick Jagger, Gordon Asher, and Prince Stanislaus Klossowski de Rola (the son of the artist Balthus), who stayed for a number of weeks and taught both Paul and me the alchemical significance of Hieronymus Bosch. One evening I was there with Paul's friend Ray Anderson when Micky Dolenz of the Monkees arrived. Later, he would recall, "Paul took us into his music room and showed us around. It has a piano painted by Dudley. That piano is the freakiest thing you've ever seen. It's lavender, gold, blue, orange—everything you could imagine—it's got millions of colors."

RIGHT: Dudley Edwards
painting Paul
McCartney's "magic"
piano, October 1966.

FAR RIGHT: Passport
portrait of the artist:
Dudley Edwards in 1967.

> **"A PSYCHEDELICALLY PAINTED PIANO IS MORE THAN THE SUM OF ITS PARTS. IT'S AN ART THAT IS SOPHISTICATED AND POETICAL, TOO.'"** Nicole Rudick, the *Paris Review*

Another special moment I remember is having early breakfast with Nico from the Velvet Underground, or the time when John Lennon called around and Paul asked if I minded if he and John retired to his music studio to do some work on a number. Eventually they emerged to play me the first rendition of "Getting Better"—I guess they wanted a layman's opinion.

Some nights we would go down to Abbey Road, where I witnessed many tracks being laid for *Sgt. Pepper*. On occasion, Paul's particular skills wouldn't require the others' attendance, for example the French horn sequence in the title track, where around twelve classical musicians assembled in two rows facing Paul with the baton. The first rendition sounded perfect to my untrained ear, but no, Paul said the second musician from the left was slightly out. The player nodded in agreement. This went on, take after take, Paul correcting one player then another until they got it right.

On another occasion I would also witness John remonstrating with the engineers in the recording booth: just because tape hadn't been cut up, reassembled, and then played backward before, he reasoned, there was no reason not to try it now.

One morning on the way back from the studio, a policeman pulled us over. Paul seemed nervous. He got out of the car to speak, and I could hear the policeman say, "Sorry sir, I didn't realize it was you." Paul later explained that it could go both ways: they'd either treat him like royalty or throw the book at him.

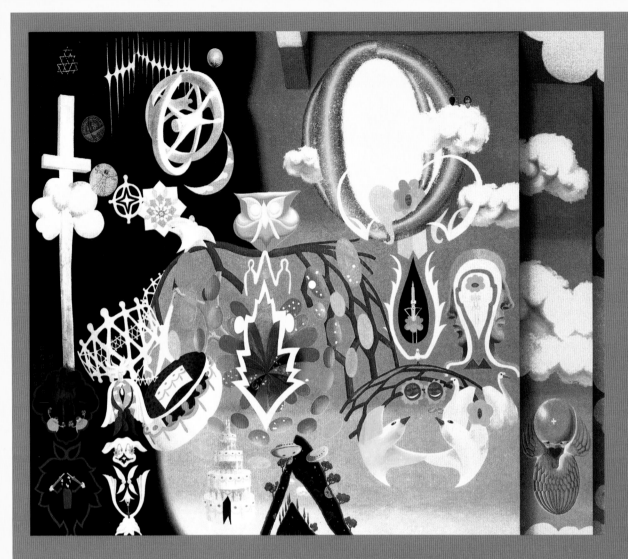

When the first complimentary copies of *Sgt. Pepper* were sent out, Paul would share some of the initial responses with me, including a letter from Karlheinz Stockhausen, congratulating him on "A Day in the Life."

Some evenings, we would visit various nightclubs around London, and it was at one of these, the Bag O' Nails, that Paul first met Linda, who would later recall riding home in a Mini with Lulu and me, and how she had been impressed to see Paul's Magrittes.

Paul had some of the best Magrittes I'd ever seen; one in particular sticks in my memory. It depicts a fish in a prison cell, pining for the sea, which can be seen in the distance, through the barred cell window.

It was through studying these paintings, coupled with an awakened interest in spirituality care of Stanislaus (aka Stash) that my work began to take on a different turn—one I expressed in my next mural, to be painted on the wall of Ringo's game room in Weybridge.

of Sgt. Pepper and his band," Lennon later said, though he conceded, "It works, because we *said* it worked, and that's how the album appeared."

"Paul was going on about this idea of some fictitious band," Harrison recalled. "That side of it didn't really interest me, other than the title song and the album cover." For Starr, "After we'd done the original 'Sgt. Pepper' song, we dropped the whole military idea. We just went on doing tracks."

As the album's opening track, "Sgt. Pepper" provides the perfect entry point into the Beatles' new, colorful world. It is a straightforward rock song, the only studio embellishment being the echo applied to the vocals. And the spotlight is firmly on McCartney, who provided a powerful lead vocal, lead guitar, and bass. Lennon and Harrison provided harmony vocals; Harrison also played guitar, and Starr drums. Four French horns were overdubbed to emphasize the idea that this was a brass band.

The song really came to life with the decision that the track should give the illusion of being a live performance: Sgt. Pepper's show. The EMI Studios sound archive would be plundered for the appropriate sound effects: the orchestra warming up at the Beatles' own session

for "A Day in the Life"; applause and laughter from recordings of audiences at London's Royal Albert Hall, the Queen Elizabeth Hall, and a live recording of the comedy show *Beyond the Fringe*, originally recorded by Martin at London's Fortune Theatre in 1961; and screams from one of the Beatles' performances at the Hollywood Bowl. An audience laugh was dropped in during an instrumental passage, as a bit of a joke; the listener would have no idea what the audience might be laughing at.

Next up was "Good Morning Good Morning," with recording beginning on February 8. Lennon later dismissed his song, inspired by a TV commercial for cornflakes, as "a throwaway, a piece of garbage," which underrates its appeal. With its detached perspective on modern life, it's something of a livelier version of "A Day in the Life," with the song's protagonist cast as a disinterested spectator of his own day-to-day existence, trudging to and from work, the highlight of the day being a teatime viewing of the British sitcom *Meet the Wife*.

The song features the Beatles in their standard stage lineup: Harrison on lead guitar, Lennon on rhythm guitar,

McCartney on bass, and Starr on drums, with McCartney providing additional guitar as well. But however simply Lennon's songs in this period started out, they inevitably became more detailed and layered, starting with the ADT applied to his lead vocal part (McCartney and Harrison provided backing vocals). He then decided he wanted to add a horn section, mostly drawn from the instrumental combo Sounds Inc. (formerly Sounds Incorporated), and consisting of three saxophones, two trombones, and a French horn. In order to make the raucous horn line sound less conventional, Emerick "shoved the mics right down the bells of the saxes and screwed the sound up with limiters and a healthy dose of effects like flanging," resulting in a punchy, pulsating sound. "Anything to make it sound unlike brass playing," said assistant engineer Richard Lush. "It was typical John Lennon—he just wanted it to sound weird."

The most novel element of the track is the use of animal sound effects, heard at both the song's beginning (a rooster crowing, as in the commercial) and at its conclusion—the latter sequence perhaps a way of disguising that the song had no proper ending. It's been said that the

order of the animal sounds heard at the end—rooster, birds, cat, dog, horse, sheep, elephant, baying dogs, and a final chicken cluck—was arranged so that every subsequent creature could devour, or frighten, the animal before it. This clearly isn't the case—a horse is hardly going to be devoured, let alone scared, by a sheep—making it more likely that the order was random.

Work began on McCartney's introspective "Fixing a Hole" on February 9 at Regent Sound studio in central London. It was the first time the Beatles had used another British studio besides EMI (although they had previously recorded German-language versions of "I Want to Hold Your Hand" and "She Loves You" at EMI's Pathé Marconi Studios in Paris in January 1964). The move was necessitated because McCartney was anxious to get working on the song, and no studios were available at EMI. Though Martin

ABOVE: Sounds Incorporated onstage at the ABC, Northampton, February 28, 1964.

called Regent a "boxy little room," it didn't hamper the band's work; the song was completed in just two sessions (the second back at EMI).

The opening harpsichord, played by Martin, immediately gives the song a dreamy, somewhat melancholy feel, and the instrument predominates throughout. McCartney provided a highly melodic bass line, Harrison neatly punctuating the song with his guitar (McCartney also played some guitar). Starr played maracas as well as drums, and Harrison and Lennon provided backing vocals (the latter's only contribution to the song). The only additional sonic touch was double-tracking of the vocals, bass, and guitar, which gave the latter a good deal more vibrancy.

Though the title was interpreted by some to refer to using heroin, while others thought inspiration came from McCartney's home-repair jobs on his house in Scotland, McCartney himself dismissed both notions, saying it was really about letting one's inner self run free, in defiance of "all those pissy people who told you, 'Don't daydream, don't do this, don't do that.'" And if it reflected any kind of altered state, it would likely be pot.

So far, Harrison had not got much of a look-in with his songs during the sessions. And he didn't get off to a very good start with the first number he offered up, "Only a Northern Song." Legend once had it that Harrison wrote the song when an additional number was needed for the *Yellow Submarine* soundtrack, keeping an orchestra waiting in the studio while he dashed it off. In fact, work on the track began on February 13, and had no connection at that time to the animated *Yellow Submarine* film; nor was an orchestra used on the track. But it makes a better backstory for what is one of Harrison's most listless numbers, which plays off the fact that the Beatles' song publishing company was named Northern Songs, and meanders along aimlessly. "I groaned inside when I heard it," Martin wrote of the song—an opinion shared by Emerick, who called it "a weak track that we all winced at."

After spending two days working on the song, Martin told Harrison it wasn't good enough for the album, so it was put aside. The Beatles would return to it on April 20, after work on *Sgt. Pepper* was completed, with the number indeed eventually earmarked for *Yellow Submarine*. "Being for the Benefit of Mr. Kite!" is sonically one of the album's most imaginative numbers. The inspiration for the song can be tied to a specific date: January 31, when the band was in Sevenoaks, Kent, shooting the promo film for "Strawberry Fields Forever." During a break, Lennon wandered into an antique shop and bought a poster advertising a performance of Pablo Fanque's Circus Royal at Town Meadows, Rochdale, on February 14, 1843. Lennon was dismissive of the song at the time, telling the band's official biographer, Hunter Davies, "I wasn't very proud [of it] . . . I was just going through the motions because we needed a new song for *Sgt. Pepper* at that moment." But in hindsight he was more generous; shortly before his death, he told *Playboy* interviewer David Scheff that the "cosmically beautiful" poster inspired a song he now called "pure, like a painting, a pure watercolor."

That said, by his own admission Lennon didn't put much effort into the lyrics. And anyone who's seen a copy of the poster, which has been reproduced innumerable times since *Sgt. Pepper*'s release, would readily agree with Lennon that, "I hardly made up a word, just connecting the lists together. Word for word, really."

What gives the song its luster is the incredible atmosphere that was conjured up for the track. Recording began on February 17, the basic track consisting of McCartney on bass, Starr on drums, and Martin playing a harmonium (an organ you had to pump with your feet as you played, leaving him "absolutely knackered," in his recollection). Harrison, Starr, Mal Evans, and roadie Neil Aspinall each played a different harmonica. During the instrumental break, Lennon had wanted a swirling, circus-type sound to take over, but Martin was unable to play the organ fast enough to get that slightly out-of-kilter effect. He neatly resolved the problem by recording himself playing at half speed, so the organ runs would sound faster when the tape was played at full speed. Lennon also provided an oompah organ part during the break. Additional overdubs featured Hammond organ, Lowrey organ, piano (often recorded at different speeds to sound faster on playback), and McCartney's (not terribly audible) guitar. Lennon's double-tracked vocal was also recorded at a slightly slower speed, thus sounding faster on playback.

Lennon told Martin he didn't just want the listener to hear the sounds of the circus, he wanted them to *feel* the experience, to believe they were actually there, watching the somersaults and the trampoline acts and the waltzing Henry the Horse; "I want to smell the sawdust," he said. In lieu of using an actual steam organ, Martin came up with a novel approach to Lennon's request. EMI's sound library had numerous recordings of organs, though Martin found they were mostly military marches. To make them sound less conventional, he had the recordings transferred to one tape, then instructed Emerick to cut the tape into fifteen-inch pieces, throw them in the air, and re-edit them together, turning some of the strips around as he did so, so that they played backward. The final edit of this sequence, heard during the instrumental break and after Lennon sings the last verse, created an eerie and disorienting backdrop for the song, giving this particular circus show a dark and even slightly sinister feeling.

McCartney's buoyant "Lovely Rita" was inspired by his delight in learning that in America, female traffic wardens were called "meter maids"; he liked the alliterative sound of the phrase, and also felt the word "maid" had some sexual connotations (inevitably, a traffic warden named Meta who had once given McCartney a ticket came later forward saying she inspired the song; McCartney insisted there was no connection). After initially thinking of making the titular Rita a villain, he opted to take a more playful approach, casting her as an unobtainable object of desire, with a somewhat butch personality (her uniform makes her look like "a military man," and she picks up tab for dinner).

Recording began on February 23, with sonic manipulation introduced from the start. When the initial tape's first four tracks were filled up—with Harrison and Lennon playing acoustic guitars, Starr playing drums, and McCartney playing a piano treated with echo—the reduction mix to a second tape was done at a slower speed. McCartney's lead vocal was also recorded at a slower speed, as was Martin's piano solo. Martin additionally gave his solo what he called "a spot of 'wow'" by putting a piece of tape on the capstan of the tape recorder, making the sound wobble a bit, producing the kind of honky-tonk sound he felt would work in the track. When played back at full speed, the song has a brightness that makes the track positively shimmer.

The backing vocals were also treated with echo, and McCartney, Lennon, and

Harrison created an ersatz brass section by blowing through combs wrapped in hard, unforgiving EMI-regulation toilet paper. Amused by hearing their echo-laden voices as they sang, they began making various improv sounds—heavy panting, grunts, and other noises—which Martin decided to tack on to the song's ending, the piano swooping in for the final notes. McCartney also played bass on the track.

"Lucy in the Sky with Diamonds" contains some of the most evocative imagery of the album. Though tagged as a drug song—the main words in the title being the initials for LSD—Lennon always insisted the title came from a drawing done by his son, Julian (who turned four in April 1967), at nursery school, "Lucy" being one of his classmates. The dreaminess of the title made Lennon think of *Alice in Wonderland* and *Through the Looking Glass*, two of his favorite books, which he loved for their surrealistic fantasy. McCartney recalled the two trading phrases as they wrote the song, McCartney coming up with "cellophane flowers" and "newspaper taxis" and Lennon thinking of "kaleidoscope eyes." Lennon later said the girl with those eyes "was the image of the female who would someday come and save me."

THE SOUND

Under the Influence

ONE REASON THE MUSIC of the Beatles continued to develop over the course of their career was their ability to absorb and synthesize things that were happening around them, and put their own spin on them in their songs.

Their early influences were simple: rock 'n' roll by the likes of Elvis Presley, Chuck Berry, and Little Richard. As the 1960s progressed, the counterculture began to bloom and their influences became more varied, meaning the band's music naturally became more complex and interesting.

One of the more unexpected outside influences on the Beatles was Indian music. While shooting their second film, *Help!* in 1965, George Harrison had become fascinated by the Indian instruments featured in a restaurant scene. Later, when shooting moved to the Bahamas, Swami Vishnu Devananda gave copies of *The Illustrated Book of Yoga* to each Beatle. Both incidents sparked Harrison's interest in the music and culture of the East, with the results most readily seen in his songs "Norwegian Wood (This Bird Has Flown)" on *Rubber Soul*, "Love You To" on *Revolver*, "Within You

Without You" on *Sgt. Pepper*, and "The Inner Light" (the B-side of the "Lady Madonna" single). Other Beatles songs also reflected this influence; "Tomorrow Never Knows," the closing track on *Revolver*, doesn't feature any Indian instruments, but the swirling sounds and Lennon's hypnotic voice create the same kind of mesmerizing drone common in Indian ragas.

The Beach Boys were Capitol Records' biggest stars until the Beatles came along, and the band's primary composer, Brian Wilson, paid keen attention to the work of the Fab Four. When *Rubber Soul* was released, he marveled at its quality, proclaiming it "A whole album with all good stuff!" It was a somewhat ironic observation, given that the US edition was a jumble of tracks from the UK versions of *Help!* and *Rubber Soul*, but it fueled Wilson's own desire to raise the bar, and he would tell his then-wife Marilyn he was

determined to create "The greatest rock album ever made!"

That album was *Pet Sounds*. Paul McCartney and John Lennon got a preview of the record in May 1966, just prior to its UK release on June 27. McCartney was especially taken with the album, telling writer David Leaf in 1990 that it "blew me out of the water." He credited the Beach Boy's harmonies on the album with inspiring the introductory passage of "Here, There and Everywhere" on *Revolver* (the "To lead a better life" part), as well as influencing the creation of *Sgt. Pepper*, telling Leaf, "I played it to John so much that it would be difficult for him to escape the influence. If records had a director within a band, I sort of directed *Pepper*. And my influence was basically the *Pet Sounds* album."

There were other influences that were closer to home. McCartney in particular went out of his way to

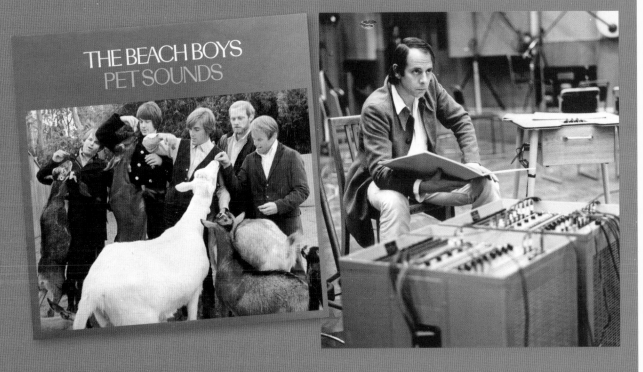

THE BEACH BOYS PET SOUNDS

investigate London's blossoming arts scene, saying in one interview, "People are saying things and painting things and writing things and composing things that are great. I *must* know what people are doing."

His interests weren't limited to music. When Brian Epstein set up a dinner with iconoclastic playwright Joe Orton, who was being considered to write a script for the Beatles' next film, McCartney was the only other Beatle in attendance. McCartney knew how to flatter an author, telling Orton, "The only thing I get from the theatre is a sore arse," then going on to praise Orton's latest play, *Loot*: "I'd've liked a bit more." Orton heard the upcoming "Penny Lane" / "Strawberry Fields Forever" single at the dinner (he preferred McCartney's song), and he admired the photo of the group chosen

for the picture sleeve, writing in his diary, "The four Beatles look different with their moustaches. Like anarchists in the early years of the century." (Epstein ended up rejecting Orton's over-the-top screenplay.)

Further influence came via the Indica Bookshop and Gallery. "We had standing orders with the Beatles, that anything interesting I should send them each one," co-owner Miles later recalled. And so the Beatles received copies of *The Fugs First Album* as well as *Freak Out!* by the Mothers of Invention; McCartney cited the latter album as another influence on *Sgt. Pepper*. It was at Indica that John Lennon picked up a copy of *The Psychedelic Experience* by Timothy Leary, which inspired the lyrics of "Tomorrow Never Knows." It was also at Indica that Lennon would meet

someone who would have a profound effect on his future life and career: Yoko Ono, who held a one-woman show at the gallery in November 1966.

McCartney, often in the company of Miles and his wife, also attended experimental music events in London. He was fascinated by the tape loops used in Luciano Berio's *Thema (Omaggio a Joyce)*, and the random sounds created by experimental group AMM, headed up by Cornelius Cardew, who'd worked with both Karlheinz Stockhausen and John Cage, two other composers whose work McCartney followed. He was just as interested in the techniques the musicians used to create their work, like Berio's tape loops, an idea that found its way into "Tomorrow Never Knows." "You don't have to like something to be influenced by it," he later explained.

> **WE DID THE WHOLE THING LIKE AN *ALICE IN WONDERLAND* IDEA, BEING IN A BOAT ON THE RIVER, SLOWLY DRIFTING DOWNSTREAM, AND THOSE GREAT CELLOPHANE FLOWERS TOWERING OVER YOUR HEAD."** Paul McCartney, 1967

After a day's rehearsal in the studio, recording began on March 1. As on "Lovely Rita," when the first four tracks of the basic rhythm tracks were full—Harrison playing an acoustic guitar and a tamboura (a stringed instrument similar to a sitar), McCartney on Lowrey organ, and Starr playing drums—the reduction mix was done at a slower speed, with Harrison's guitar given a touch of phasing. The organ stop used on the Lowrey gave it the bell-like

quality of a celeste, the song's most distinctive element, providing a lovely beginning to this ethereal tune.

Lennon recorded two lead vocals, with backing vocals by McCartney; each of their vocal parts was recorded at a slower speed and treated with echo (Martin said "Lucy" had more variations in tape speed than any other *Sgt. Pepper* track). Lennon's diction was precise: he carefully enunciated each syllable, making the words seem elongated;

LEFT: Ringo Starr, John Lennon, George Martin, and Paul McCartney during the *Pepper* sessions, March 1967.

RIGHT: The Beatles with Jimmy Nicol (*second left*) during the drummer's brief run as stand-in drummer, June 1964.

combined with a vocal melody that was largely centered on a single note, the effect was mesmerizing. Harrison's electric guitar part was distorted by sending it through a Leslie speaker (a rotating speaker in a Hammond organ)—the same thing they had done with Lennon's vocal on *Revolver*'s final track, "Tomorrow Never Knows." Only McCartney's bass was recorded straightforwardly.

Hunter Davies writes that McCartney's optimistic "Getting Better" was inspired by his memory of the Beatles' 1964 tour where session drummer Jimmy Nicol substituted for Starr, who was recovering from tonsillitis; when asked how it felt being suddenly thrust into the most popular band in the world, he'd inevitably respond, "It's getting better." McCartney played down that association, saying that his strongest

memory of writing the song was in composing the music: "That's the important bit; the casual thought that set it off isn't too important to me."

The lyrics have a positive/negative interplay similar to "We Can Work It Out," where Lennon's urgency about life being short is tempered by McCartney's insistence on a good outcome. In the new song, McCartney's declaration about things getting better is followed by Lennon's backhanded barb that it couldn't get much worse. Lennon also took the song into darker territory, contributing lines in which the narrator confesses to being abusive, saying bluntly of a former girlfriend, "I beat her." In the sunny Summer of Love, such sentiments were overlooked, but Lennon later admitted the song had an autobiographical element. "I was a hitter," he said. "I fought men and I hit

women. . . . I will have to be a lot older before I can face in public how I treated women as a youngster."

Recording began on March 9. McCartney wrote the melody at home on a piano he'd had painted in a bright, psychedelic design, something he even credited with influencing the mood of the song. "The way [the piano] was painted added to the fun of it all," he said. "It's an optimistic song." (He later had a replica of it made, taking it on the road when he began doing solo tours and dubbing it his "magic piano.") Hence keyboards are the predominant sound through the track—if played unconventionally. Martin played both a regular piano, and a pianette (an electric piano), by striking the strings of the instruments rather than playing the keys, which gave the music a decided sharpness.

ABOVE: The EMI Studios harmonium used by the Beatles on *Sgt. Pepper.*

RIGHT: George Harrison talks to Michael Nesmith of the Monkees at the session for "A Day in the Life," February 10, 1967.

THE SONG WAS WRITTEN AT KLAUS VOORMANN'S HOUSE IN HAMPSTEAD, LONDON, ONE NIGHT AFTER DINNER. . . . THE TUNE CAME FIRST, THEN THE FIRST SENTENCE . . . *WE WERE TALKING.*" George Harrison on "Within You Without You"

Along with "Sgt. Pepper," "Getting Better" is the track that sounds most like the pre-*Pepper* Beatles, with the group in the lead guitar/rhythm guitar/bass/drums formation, as well as featuring the Beatles' trademark harmonies, from McCartney, Lennon, and Harrison; even the handclaps harken back to the era of Beatlemania. But along with keyboard lines, Harrison added another unusual flavor to the track with his droning tamboura, while Starr also played congas. The vocals were double-tracked, but there were no other experiments in varying the sound, such as recording at a slower speed.

COLOR AND SOUND

In his memoir on working with the Beatles, Geoff Emerick writes that recording sessions involving Harrison's songs were "approached differently. . . . It was never said in so many words, but there was a feeling that his songs simply didn't have the integrity of John's or Paul's . . . and so no one was prepared to expend very much time or effort on them." Given that attitude, it's perhaps not surprising Harrison is the only Beatle to play on "Within You Without You," his songwriting contribution to *Sgt. Pepper*.

Harrison had written the song in the wake of an evening spent with one of the Beatles' longtime friends Klaus Voormann, whom they'd met when they first played Hamburg, Germany, in 1960, and who later designed the cover of *Revolver*; in fact, he'd begun the song while still at Voormann's home, playing a pedal harmonium.

Harrison had previously played various Indian instruments on Beatles recordings, including a number of tracks on *Sgt. Pepper*, but "Within You Without You" was the first time a Beatles song had been so thoroughly steeped in the music of the East. Harrison and Aspinall played tamboura, and Harrison also played acoustic guitar and sitar. But most of the musicians who played the more exotic instruments on the track came from London's Asian Music Circle, playing sitar, tamboura, dilruba (a stringed instrument played with a bow), swarmandal (an Indian harp), and a tabla (a drum shaped somewhat like bongos). They also provided atmosphere along with their instruments, unrolling carpets so they could sit comfortably on the floor and lighting incense.

"Suddenly we had color, life, and warmth in our normally cold and featureless surroundings," said Martin.

It was Harrison who was in charge when recording began on March 15, singing the parts he wanted the musicians to play. But it was Martin who provided the other major element in the song by writing and arranging music for the accompanying string section (eight violins and three cellos). It was a challenge for the players; the dilruba played the song's melody, and the string players had a hard time matching their own playing with the more sinuous rhythms of the Indian musicians.

No one had ever heard Indian instruments recorded with such depth and clarity on what was ostensibly a Western pop song before. The droning tambouras set the stage for the melody to emerge, as the swarmandal provides a gently cascading series of notes before the tabla comes in. The melody of Harrison's double-tracked vocal is matched by the dilrubas, two of them made even more elastic by having been recorded at a faster speed, so they sounded slower on playback. The violins and cellos come in gradually, almost unnoticeably at first, blossoming fully during the instrumental break, when the Eastern and Western instruments begin winding around each other, blending together

The Eternal Debate: Mono vs. Stereo

SGT. PEPPER WAS THE LAST Beatles album to be released in mono and stereo on both sides of the Atlantic. By the 1970s, mono albums were no longer being manufactured, and the Beatles mono recordings went out of print.

When the Beatles first began making records in 1962, most people had mono record players. It wasn't thought that pop or rock music would benefit from being recorded in stereo. Stereo was the province of classical, jazz, or easy-listening recordings—the kind of records listened to by people who had the money to buy expensive hi-fidelity systems. Accordingly, more mono records were manufactured than stereo recordings. And more time was spent on making the mono mixes.

The Beatles themselves were more interested in the mono mixes, and were often present at the sessions when their songs were being mixed in mono. "The only real version of *Sgt. Pepper's Lonely Hearts Club Band* is the mono version," Richard Lush told Beatles historian Mark Lewisohn. "The Beatles were there for all the mono mixes. Then, after the album was finished, George Martin, Geoff [Emerick], and I did the stereo in

a few days, just the three of us, without a Beatle in sight."

Mono and stereo mixes also weren't necessarily done at the same time, meaning differences could crop up in different mixes of the same song. This is true of every Beatles album (and a few singles) for which there were mono and stereo mixes. Some of the more readily apparent differences on *Sgt. Pepper* include:

- "Sgt. Pepper's Lonely Hearts Club Band." On the mono version, the lead guitar is louder in the last verse, and there's a longer pause between the final chord played by the French horns and the screaming fans.
- "She's Leaving Home." The mono version runs faster and is a semitone higher in pitch than the mono version (giving it a running time of 3:26 versus 3:35 for the stereo version).
- "Being for the Benefit of Mr. Kite!"

The swirling organ effects during the instrumental break are different in each version.

- "Within You Without You." The laughter at the end of song is different in each version.
- "Sgt. Pepper (Reprise)." The segue from the chicken cluck of "Good Morning Good Morning" to the opening guitar of "Sgt. Pepper" isn't as smooth on the mono version. The mono version also has some audience laughter at the beginning and a vocal line from Paul McCartney after the final verse that's much louder. The segue into "A Day in the Life" is also different in each version.

Some differences you'll have to listen harder for. On "Lucy in the Sky with Diamonds," for example, there's a lot more echo on the mono version, which gives the song a more languorous feel, but that doesn't stand out as much as

the difference in pitch between the mono and stereo versions of "She's Leaving Home."

In Emerick's view, the stereo version of *Sgt. Pepper* has "an unnecessary surfeit of panning and effects like ADT . . . Richard and I would sometimes get carried away with them because of their novelty value—especially if George Martin wasn't there to rebuke us."

Whether the differences make one version better than the other is a subject of much debate, especially online. Some feel the mono mix has a greater power, while others like the cleaner sound of the stereo mix. It's a matter of personal taste.

The Beatles (also known as "The White Album"), released in 1968, was the last Beatles album issued in mono,

though not in the US, as Capitol was phasing out mono records. The mono version of the *Yellow Submarine* soundtrack, released in 1969, isn't a true mono mix; it's "fold down" mono, wherein the right and left channels of the stereo mix are combined to make a mono recording, with one exception: the *Sgt. Pepper* reject "Only a Northern Song." When work on the song was completed in April 1967, only a mono mix had been made. The following year, when the song was remixed for the *Yellow Submarine* film, that mono mix was used, instead of the original four-track tapes. Hence, it's the only true mono mix on the mono *Yellow Submarine*. On the stereo edition of the album, an "artificially enhanced" stereo version is used.

Mono reissues of *Sgt. Pepper* did appear over the years. The album was a part of the 1982 boxed set *The Beatles: Mono Collection*, marking the first time the mono *Sgt. Pepper* had been available since its original release. The same year, a mono version of the album was released on red vinyl in Japan; in 2003, there was another mono reissue of the album in Japan. The most recent releases of *Sgt. Pepper* in mono are in the 2009 CD boxed set *The Beatles in Mono* and the 2014 vinyl boxed set of the same name. And while the 2012 stereo vinyl releases used digital masters created for the 2009 reissues of the albums, the 2014 mono vinyl records used the original tapes, meaning the 2014 box is a true analog release.

beautifully. Harrison's lyric placed him in the position of teacher, preaching the wisdom of looking beyond ego and discovering one's own inner light. It was an attitude that some found hectoring. Harrison, perhaps realizing this, had some laughter overdubbed at the song's ending, as a way of lightening the song's mood.

FINISHING TOUCHES

The *Daily Mail* had proved to be an unlikely muse for *Sgt. Pepper*. Lennon had drawn on two of its stories for "A Day in the Life," and now McCartney found inspiration in an article that ran in the paper on February 27, headlined "A-level girl dumps car and vanishes." The young woman in question was Melanie Coe, then seventeen, who ran away from her home in Stamford Hill, London. "I cannot imagine why she should run away," her father was quoted as saying in the story. "She has everything here."

McCartney used this as a jumping off point for his own reflection on the generation gap, "She's Leaving Home," detailing the story of a young woman leaving home in search of freedom and fun. Lennon provided what McCartney called the "Greek chorus"—the answering lines from the parents' point of view, capped by the realization that fun is "the one thing that money can't buy."

McCartney and Lennon are the only Beatles to appear on the track, and even then only vocally; McCartney wanted the music played on classical instruments. This ended up causing some bad feeling between McCartney and his producer, when Martin wasn't immediately available to write the arrangement and McCartney tapped Mike Leander, whom he knew of due

OPPOSITE: A *Daily Mirror* article about the girl who "has everything" that inspired Paul McCartney to write "She's Leaving Home."

ABOVE LEFT: Marianne Faithfull, whose work with Mike Leander brought the arranger to the attention of Paul McCartney.

ABOVE RIGHT: Journalist Hunter Davies, who wrote the authorized biography *The Beatles* in 1968.

to Leander's work with singer Marianne Faithfull, for the job. Unusually, McCartney simply met with Leander and told him what he wanted, leaving Leander to go off and do the writing on his own (in contrast to how, for example, McCartney had sung the trumpet solo he wanted for "Penny Lane" to Martin, who then wrote it down at the same time). Leander wrote a score for four violins, two violas, two cellos, a double bass, and a harp (the latter of which would be played by Sheila Bromberg, the first woman to appear on a Beatles record).

Martin was hurt McCartney hadn't waited until he was free to write the arrangement himself, but he would still nonetheless serve as the producer for the March 17 session with good grace. In 1993, he got some of his own back

in his book *With a Little Help from My Friends: The Making of Sgt. Pepper*, taking a little swipe by calling Leander's score "a good workmanlike job" but going on to say the harp part was "too tinkly" and the strings "a shade too lush." It's not a bad assessment; in contrast to the more minimalist strings on "Yesterday" or "Eleanor Rigby," the score for "She's Leaving Home"— especially the flowery harp part—feels overwrought.

McCartney's lead vocal cast him as a sympathetic narrator, much as he'd been in "Eleanor Rigby." It's one of his most moving performances, particularly when he soars up to the high note during the chorus on the word "home." McCartney and Lennon's vocals were also double-tracked during the chorus, filling out the sound.

> " I PLAYED CHESS WITH THE ROADIES ALL THROUGH MAKING [*SGT. PEPPER*]. THERE WAS A LOT OF TIME THAT THE GENIUSES WERE PUTTING ON HARMONIES AND ORCHESTRAS, SO THE TRACK WOULD BE DONE AS FAR AS I WAS CONCERNED, AND I'D HAVE TO WAIT DAYS TO PUT A TAMBOURINE ON." Ringo Starr, 2008

The sessions were nearly over, but no song had yet been written for Starr to sing. Finally, on March 28, they began working on a song with a working title of "Bad Finger Boogie," which would later take on the name of its chorus line: "With a Little Help from My Friends." Biographer Hunter Davies was invited to McCartney's home on March 29 and watched him and Lennon in the process of working on the song prior to its first recording session that night. The two Beatles sat in McCartney's work room at the top of the house, playing their instruments, singing proposed lines, breaking off and playing raucous renditions of other songs, and then returning to the project at hand.

Starr wasn't the strongest singer, and Lennon and McCartney tailored the song to his vocal range. In fact, the song takes his singing ability as its starting point, having him somewhat mournfully ask if singing out of tune would make the audience walk out. (The line had originally asked if the listener would throw tomatoes at the hapless singer—a line Starr stoutly refused to sing.) But the overall premise is positive; whatever life's ills, he can always rely on his friends. It was a sweet and simple sentiment, well suited to the

man who'd previously tapped into the kiddie market with the sing-along "Yellow Submarine" (presaging the success he'd find as the narrator of the *Thomas the Tank Engine and Friends* animated TV series). Being the Beatles, they snuck in a little innuendo as well, during the call-and-response about what you see when you turn out the light; Starr can't say, but teasingly adds, "I know it's mine." And, of course, "getting high" lends itself to different interpretations.

Aside from ADT on the vocals, there were no other sonic embellishments. Harrison played guitar, McCartney played bass and piano, Starr played drums, and Lennon played the cowbell. It had been decided that the track would follow the opening "Sgt. Pepper," which ends with McCartney introducing the first "act," Billy Shears. That meant the band had to record a fuller introduction, singing the name "Bill-ly Shears!" while Martin added what he called a "smidgen" of Hammond organ.

Work on the album was now wrapping up. McCartney was due to leave for America on April 3, where he planned to surprise his girlfriend, actress Jane Asher, who was touring the US with the Bristol Old Vic, by showing up for her

twenty-first birthday on April 5. So the last major recording session for *Sgt. Pepper* came on April 1. Neil Aspinall had suggested that, since the album was supposed to emulate a live show, why not have Sgt. Pepper's band return at the end? Hence the reprise of the title track, which runs to 1:19, and which the band nailed down in one eleven-hour session. It's another number using the Harrison, lead guitar; Lennon, rhythm guitar; McCartney, bass; Starr, drums lineup (with McCartney also playing organ and Starr additional percussion), and has the most "live and in concert" sound of the album. There's a real exuberance in the track, too, due to its having been recorded in the larger Studio One; as Martin later wrote, "the electrifying, football stadium atmosphere comes through." There were no reduction mixes; the song was entirely recorded on one four-track tape.

Martin came up with *Sgt. Pepper's* running order. In the days of the two-sided album, his goal was to open and close each side with a strong track. "Sgt. Pepper" was the obvious opener, naturally seguing into "With a Little Help from My Friends." "Lucy in the Sky with Diamonds" comes next, due to its entirely different sound compared

ABOVE: Geoff Emerick
(*left*) and Ringo Starr
with the former's
Grammy Award for Best
Engineered Recording
(Non-Classical), which he
won for his work on *Sgt.
Pepper*, March 8, 1968.

ABOVE RIGHT: Emerick
works the EMI Studios
mixing desk while Brian
Epstein (*top left*) and
George Martin look on.

to its predecessor. The more positively oriented "Getting Better" and "Fixing a Hole" follow, each providing a balance to the poignancy of "She's Leaving Home," before the phantasmagoria of "Being for the Benefit of Mr. Kite!" brings "Act One" to a colorful close.

Martin was baffled as to where to place "Within You Without You," deciding it would open side two as a matter of default; it didn't seem to match up well with anything else on the album. It was the laughter Harrison had placed at the end of the song that led

Martin to decide the jokey "When I'm Sixty-Four" would follow it. He also admitted he'd never particularly taken to "Lovely Rita," and so had the song come next, "as a bit of padding." "Good Morning Good Morning" follows because the final cluck led so nicely into the opening guitar line on the "Sgt. Pepper" reprise, which then segues into "A Day in the Life." (Interestingly, at one point there was a different proposed running order for side one: "Sgt. Pepper," "With a Little Help from My Friends," "Being for the Benefit of Mr. Kite!,"

LEFT: John Lennon relaxes at home with a copy of the *International Times*, April 1967.

"Fixing a Hole," "Lucy in the Sky with Diamonds," "Getting Better," "She's Leaving Home.")

It seemed that nothing could follow the imposing final chord of "A Day in the Life." But the Beatles had one final ace up their sleeves. There was a space between that last chord and the run-out groove of the vinyl album; why not fill it with something? Lennon had the idea to add a fifteen-kilohertz tone after the chord faded away—a frequency only audible to a dog.

It was also decided to place a short clip of some sort of noise at the very end of the record; if you didn't have an automatic turntable, then the clip would repeat endlessly until the turntable's tone arm was picked up. So, on April 21, the Beatles gathered in the studio one more time and were recorded babbling away: "They made funny noises, said random things; just nonsense," Emerick recalled. A short sequence of gibberish was extracted and edited onto the mono and stereo masters. Those who mined the group's albums for hidden messages of significance were delighted to find that when spinning the record backward, this end sequence appeared to be saying, "We'll fuck you like you're superman."

Capitol Records, which released the Beatles' records in America, wasn't impressed; neither the fifteen-kilohertz tone, or the gibberish, appeared on US editions of the album. Subsequent non-US re-pressings of the album also omit these final aural jokes; they were finally restored when *Sgt. Pepper* was reissued on its twentieth anniversary in 1987.

And so, nearly five months after they'd entered the studio in November 1966, work on *Sgt. Pepper's Lonely Hearts Club Band* was finally completed. The album's release was six weeks away.

> " I JUST LISTENED TO IT AND SAID TO MYSELF, 'GOD, I REALLY LOVE THIS ALBUM.' STILL, TODAY, IT JUST SOUNDS SO FRESH. IT SOUNDS FULL OF IDEAS. I HAVEN'T HEARD ANYTHING THIS YEAR THAT'S AS INVENTIVE. I DON'T REALLY EXPECT TO." Paul McCartney, 1987

"**SGT. PEPPER'S LONELY HEARTS CLUB BAND** WAS A MUSICAL FRAGMENTATION GRENADE, EXPLODING WITH A FORCE THAT IS STILL BEING FELT. IT GRABBED THE WORLD OF POP MUSIC BY THE SCRUFF OF THE NECK, SHOOK IT HARD, AND LEFT IT TO WANDER OFF, DIZZY BUT WAGGING ITS TAIL." George Martin

Sgt. Pepper would hold a unique position in the band's catalogue; they never released another album quite like it. "On *Sgt. Pepper*, we had more instruments and instrumentation than we have ever had, and more orchestral stuff than we have ever used before," McCartney said at the time of its release. This was certainly true, but it wasn't the only thing that made *Sgt. Pepper* different. More than any other Beatles album, it created a highly specialized environment. This is what underlies the "concept" idea of the album; in inviting the listener to Sgt. Pepper's show, the Beatles were also extending an invitation to step into a colorful new world.

It was the first time a Beatles album was specifically designed to be listened to all the way through, like a classical piece. There are no pauses between the songs, as on a standard album; the Beatles asked that such "banding" not be used, while both of the "Sgt. Pepper" numbers crossfade into the next song. The subject matter, too, was different. Where boy-meets-girl/boy-loses-girl songs had once dominated the group's repertoire, most of the songs on the album address other concerns. There is a mature acknowledgment of the emotional complexities of the world. While there are songs of optimism ("With a Little Help from My Friends," "Getting Better"), there are others about loss ("She's Leaving Home") and the mundanity of modern life ("Good Morning Good Morning"); even the chipper mood of "When I'm Sixty-Four" masks an underlying fear of loneliness and death. "Lucy in the Sky with Diamonds" and "Being for the Benefit of Mr. Kite!" are the Beatles' most imaginative flights of fancy. And "A Day in the Life" is surely the band's most powerful piece of work.

The Beatles were prime movers in transforming rock 'n' roll into rock; with *Sgt. Pepper*, they transformed rock into art.

"*Sgt. Pepper's Lonely Hearts Club Band* is one of the most important steps in this group's career," Lennon said at the press preview for the album, held in mid-May. "It had to be just right. We tried and I think succeeded in achieving what we set out to do."

And succeed they did, beyond their wildest expectations.

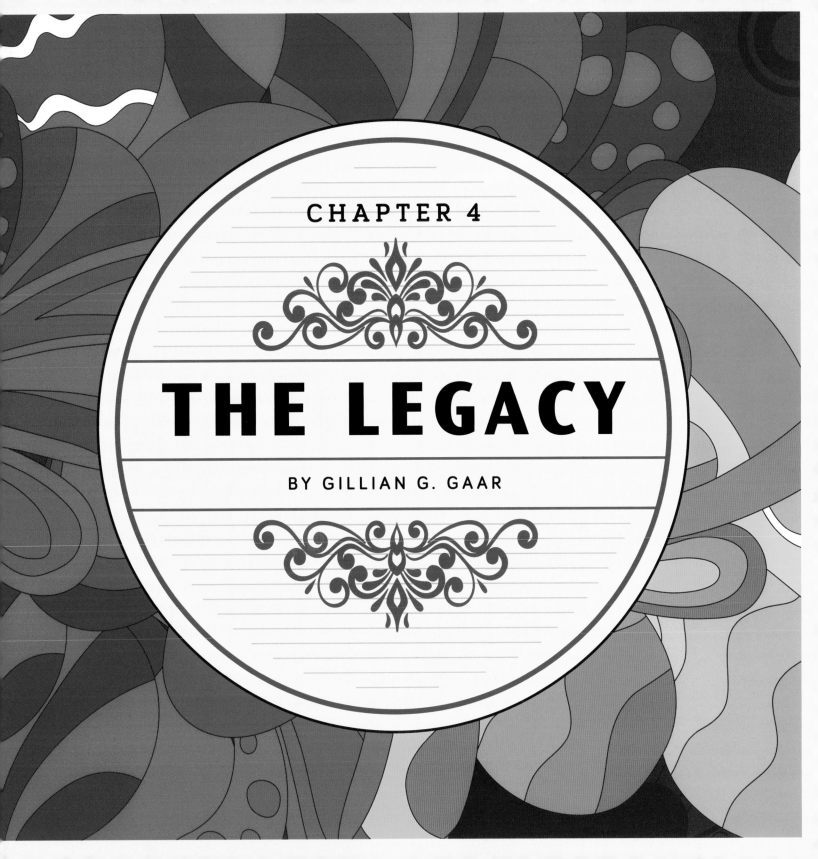

CHAPTER 4

THE LEGACY

BY GILLIAN G. GAAR

"See, I never really liked *Sgt. Pepper*. I mean, I think it's a fine album. All the work we do is fine. But I think I felt like a session man on it."

Ringo Starr to *Inner-View*, 1977

SGT. PEPPER was the most hotly anticipated release of 1967. The official release dates were June 1 in the UK and June 2 in the US, ten long months after the Beatles' last new studio album, *Revolver*. (Other accounts have the album being released, in the UK at least, as early as May 24, but June 1 is the most widely accepted date.)

This was an unprecedentedly long time between albums for any musical act at that point—from 1963 to 1965, the Beatles had always released two albums a year—prompting speculation that the group's creative well had run dry and that they were on the verge of breaking up. The band's official fan magazine, *The Beatles Monthly Book*, felt the necessity of publishing an article entitled "Recording: Why It Takes So Long" in its April 1967 issue to assure fans that all was well in the Beatles camp, with Beatles aides Neil Aspinall and Mal Evans pointing to the length of time now spent in the studio working out songs and arrangements, and experimenting with different recording techniques.

Paul McCartney couldn't wait to reveal the ace the Beatles had up their sleeve. "I remember the great glee seeing in one of the papers how the Beatles have dried up, there's nothing come from them, they're stuck in the studio, they can't think what they're doing, and I was sitting rubbing my hands, saying 'You just wait,'" he later recalled.

Select friends were given sneak peaks. When the Byrds' David Crosby dropped by the studio while the album was being recorded, the band arranged for "A Day in the Life" to be cued up. While in America in April, visiting his girlfriend Jane Asher, McCartney played "A Day in the Life" for Jefferson Airplane while hanging out with them in San Francisco. "I totally, literally did not know what to say, except 'Fuckin' great!'" said Marty Balin. While in Los Angeles, McCartney played the track for the Beach Boys' Brian Wilson, as well as John and Michelle Phillips of the Mamas & the Papas; the *NME* subsequently wrote, "Brian Wilson is reported to have heard the Beatles LP track 'A Day in the Life Of' [sic] and to be so knocked out that he has retired to live in a sauna bath, there to sweat out some more mind-jamming material for further Beach Boys discs." McCartney also played "She's Leaving Home" on the piano, moving Wilson's then-wife, Marilyn, to tears.

The first public airing of *Sgt. Pepper* was thoroughly in keeping with the freewheeling spirit of the times. After the album was finished in mid-April, the Beatles turned up at the Chelsea flat of the Mamas' Cass Elliott on a Sunday morning, put her stereo on a window ledge, and began playing an acetate of *Sgt. Pepper*. "The music blasted through the neighborhood," Aspinall recalled.

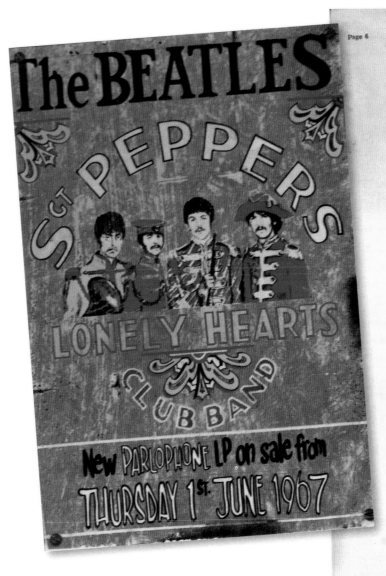

PREVIOUS SPREAD:
Performers dressed in
Sgt. Pepper suits march
through the stadium
during the opening
ceremony of the London
2012 Olympic Games,
July 27, 2012.

ABOVE: A promotional
poster (*left*) and an
International Times ad
(*right*) announcing the
release of *Sgt. Pepper*.

"All the windows around us opened and people leaned out, wondering. It was obvious who it was on the record. Nobody complained. . . . People were smiling and giving us the thumbs up."

Further illicit airings followed. In Los Angeles, various radio stations began broadcasting select tracks in May, and pirate station Radio London played the record in its entirety on May 12. The first official broadcast came eight days later, when the album was played on Kenny Everett's *Where It's At* show on the BBC Light Programme; by then, the BBC's censors had stepped in and banned "A Day in the Life" due to its drug references.

A special listening party for top journalists and DJs was held on May 19 at the home of Beatles manager Brian Epstein. There was some concern that

the album might be too great a leap for some fans—in August, *The Beatles Monthly Book* would run an article entitled, "Is *Sgt. Pepper* Too Advanced for the Average Pop Fan to Appreciate?"— so the Beatles were also on hand at the party to charm the press.

"The people who bought our records in the past must realize we couldn't go on making the same type forever," John Lennon told the *NME*. "We must change and I believe people know this." George Harrison was equally forthright with *Disc*. "We're not trying to outwit the public. The whole idea is to try a little bit to lead people into different tastes. Then, the people with enough intelligence to understand what we're trying to do will get some pleasure."

A few reviews expressed some perplexity. *NME* cautiously wrote,

ABOVE LEFT: The Beatles present their new LP at the press launch for the album, held at the Belgravia home of Brian Epstein, May 19, 1967.

ABOVE: McCartney greets an autograph-hunting fan outside his home on Cavendish Avenue, London.

OPPOSITE: *International Times* gives its view on *Sgt. Pepper*.

> **"*SGT. PEPPER'S LONELY HEARTS CLUB BAND* IS AS FLIPPED AS ITS TITLE IMPLIES. TRIPPING WITH THIS RECORD IS A MIND-BLOWING EXPERIENCE. THE RECORD IS A CONTINUUM OF FANTASTIC SOUND."** *International Times* review of the album

"Whether the album is their best yet, I wouldn't like to say after one hearing. . . . But it is a very good LP and will sell like hot cakes." Most notoriously, the *New York Times* gave the album a decidedly mixed review. "Like an over-attended child, *Sgt. Pepper* is spoiled," Richard Goldstein wrote. "The Beatles have given us an album of special effects, dazzling but ultimately fraudulent." The resulting uproar was such that Goldstein was moved to write a follow-up that appeared in the *Village Voice*, though he refused to back down from his earlier assessment: "Much of the radicalism on *Sgt. Pepper* has appeared elsewhere, in a less sophisticated form. . . . *Sgt. Pepper* is not a work of plagiarism, but neither does it represent a breakthrough."

Most of the media were fulsome in their praise, however. In the UK, *Record Retailer* called the album "a sensational album which will be their biggest seller yet," adding that each song could be released as a single in its own right. In the *Sunday Times*, Derek Jewell called the album "remarkable . . . a tremendous advance even in the increasingly adventurous progress of the Beatles," delighting in the "splendid urban poetry" of the lyrics. In the *Times*, critic Kenneth Tynan lauded the album's

release as "a decisive moment in the history of Western civilization."

Stateside, the reviews were generally just as effusive, *Time* calling *Sgt. Pepper* "a historic departure in the progress of music—any music," while in *Newsweek* Jack Kroll compared the album to Edith Sitwell's *Façade*, and "A Day in the Life" to T. S. Eliot's "The Waste Land": "a superb achievement of their brilliant and startlingly effective popular art." And if some *Monthly Book* readers complained that the band "ought to stop being so clever and give us tunes we can enjoy," there were far many more who approved: "*Sgt. Pepper* contains words and ideas which are far above anything anyone else is capable of creating."

Sgt. Pepper became an immediate best seller, topping charts around the world. But its impact went well beyond its commercial success. "Musically its conquest was total," Philip Norman later wrote in his Beatles biography *Shout!* "It equally entranced the most avant-garde and most cautious, both fan and foe alike."

It was more than just the release of an album, it was an event, a rallying cry to youth around the world. "The closest Western civilization has come to unity since the Congress of Vienna in 1815

was the week the *Sgt. Pepper* album was released," future *Rolling Stone* scribe Langdon Winner wrote in 1968. "At the time I happened to be driving across country on Interstate 80. In each city where I stopped for gas or food— Laramie, Ogallala, Moline, South Bend—the melodies wafted in from some far-off transistor radio or portable hi-fi. It was the most amazing thing I'd ever heard. For a brief while the irreparably fragmented consciousness of the West was unified, at least in the minds of the young."

It was thus the perfect album to usher in the Summer of Love. The first public stamp of approval came on June 4, when the Jimi Hendrix Experience

LEFT: George Harrison, John Lennon, Brian Epstein, and Paul McCartney at Abbey Road for the live broadcast of *Our World*, June 25, 1967.

performed at London's Saville Theatre (then being leased by Beatles manager Brian Epstein) and opened their set with *Sgt. Pepper's* title track, as an astonished McCartney and Harrison looked on. "That was like the ultimate compliment," McCartney later said. "I put that down as one of the great honors of my career."

WELCOME TO OUR WORLD

The Beatles' stature as global ambassadors for goodwill was sealed on June 25, when they performed "All You Need Is Love" on *Our World*, the first live global television broadcast, transmitted to twenty-four different countries. The performance was like a scaled-down version of the "A Day in the Life" session: there was a thirteen-piece orchestra; celebrity guests like Mick Jagger, Marianne Faithfull, Eric Clapton, and Keith Moon were in attendance; EMI's Studio One was festively decorated with streamers, balloons, and placards that spelled out the song's title in a number of different languages; with the Beatles and their friends all sporting the height of psychedelic fashion.

Not everyone was as eager to climb aboard the bandwagon. The BBC had been quick to ban "A Day in the Life" due to its purported drug references, and with the album's lyrics printed in full on the cover, those who were similarly inclined to find hidden meanings in the Beatles' songs were able to do so. Most famously, "Lucy in the Sky with Diamonds" was said to

> **WE HAD BEEN TOLD WE'D BE SEEN RECORDING IT BY THE WHOLE WORLD AT THE SAME TIME. SO WE HAD ONE MESSAGE FOR THE WORLD: LOVE. WE NEED MORE LOVE IN THE WORLD."** Paul McCartney

refer to LSD (something Lennon consistently denied in interviews up to his death), but a censorious finger was also pointed at other songs: "Fixing a Hole" must refer to shooting up; "Henry the horse" in "Being for the Benefit of Mr. Kite!" was surely another coded reference to heroin; and the invitation to have some "tea" in "Lovely Rita" had to

RIGHT: Mick Jagger and John Lennon at Abbey Road, June 25, 1967.

FAR RIGHT: Lennon gets ready for "Love."

be a reference to pot. Even as late as 1970, US vice president Spiro Agnew was still beating the anti-drug drum, saying of "With a Little Help from My Friends," "It's a catchy tune, but until it was pointed out to me, I never realized that the 'friends' were assorted drugs."

That drugs did have influence during the creation of the album is undeniable (though McCartney would insist that it was pot that had the upper hand, not acid). But phrases like "getting high" and "turn you on" were used more as in-jokes, playful double entendre; the intent wasn't to proselytize.

Further out on the fringes of rationality were those who imbued the Beatles with otherworldly powers. In his 1968 essay "Thank God for the Beatles," the psychologist and LSD proponent Timothy Leary described the Beatles as "evolutionary agents sent by God, endowed with a mysterious power to create a new human species." He further wrote that *Sgt. Pepper* was specifically designed to be experienced while under the influence of drugs, calling it "the most powerful brainwashing device our planet has ever known." Indeed, if you were an observer from a

more highly evolved planet wondering how to change human psychology and human cultural development (in other words if you were a divine messenger), would you not inevitably combine electrical energies from outside with biochemical catalysts inside to accomplish your mutation?"

Others divined hidden meanings in the Beatles' work, even suggesting that Paul McCartney had died in a car accident in 1966 and been replaced by a double (see page 88). Lennon routinely dismissed such interpretations of the Beatles' work. When asked about the

"Paul is dead" rumors by *Rolling Stone*, he shrugged, "Some people have got nothing better to do than study Bibles and make myths about it. . . . It's just something for them to do. They live vicariously." But it was a sign of how thoroughly *Sgt. Pepper* permeated the pop-culture landscape. The cover art was quickly emulated (on the Rolling Stones' *Their Satanic Majesties Request*) and parodied (the Mothers of Invention's *We're Only in It for the Money* the first of innumerable iterations). But its musical impact would be more profound.

HERE, THERE, AND EVERYWHERE

In his review of the album in the *Village Voice*, Tom Phillips called *Sgt. Pepper* "a breakthrough. . . . Specifically, I think they've turned the record-album itself into an art-form." Pop's parameters had been permanently expanded. When the Small Faces headed into the studio at the end of 1967 to record *Ogdens' Nut Gone Flake* (released the following year), there was a new sense of restraints being broken. "In studios back then you'd have a grand piano, tubular bells, tympani, harpsichord, celeste, you might have a Theremin,

ABOVE: Promotional posters advertising the film adaptations of a pair of concept albums by the Who: *Tommy* (1975) and *Quadrophenia* (1979).

OPPOSITE, RIGHT: *Days of Future Passed*, the 1967 Moody Blues album for which the London Festival Orchestra received equal billing.

OPPOSITE, FAR RIGHT: Pink Floyd's 1973 LP *The Dark Side of the Moon*.

a Mellotron," the band's Ian McLagan later told *Mojo*. "We had the time, and we had the songs, and we didn't have to be guitar/bass/organ/drums any more. We were given space."

The Moody Blues' *Days of Future Passed*, recorded during the same period, one-upped "A Day in the Life" by using the London Festival Orchestra throughout the album, and even name-checking the orchestra on the cover. Bands felt freer to indulge themselves while making records, whether it was using a wider variety of instruments not typically associated with rock in recording their songs, releasing double albums to make a fuller statement of where they stood artistically, or releasing a record in a gatefold sleeve, even if it was a single album.

Sgt. Pepper also boosted the profile of the concept album. The Beatles didn't invent the concept album; critics have pointed to records like Frank Sinatra's *In the Wee Small Hours*, and, in the rock era, the Beach Boys' *Pet Sounds*, the Kinks' *Face to Face*, and the Mother of Invention's *Freak Out!* as earlier examples of a record with a narrative theme. But none of them enjoyed the commercial success of *Sgt. Pepper*, which naturally helped popularize the "concept album" idea. From there, it was a small step from concept album to full-fledged rock opera, from *The Who Sell Out* to *Tommy* and *Quadrophenia*. Thus the groundwork was laid for innumerable permutations of what a "concept album" could mean: Pink Floyd's *Dark Side of the Moon* and *The Wall*; David Bowie's *The Rise and Fall of Ziggy Stardust and the Spiders from Mars*; Queensrÿche's *Operation: Mindcrime*; Green Day's *American Idiot*; Kate Bush's *50 Words for Snow*.

But *Sgt. Pepper* also cast a shadow over the rest of the Beatles' career. In 1975, *NME* critic Nick Kent observed,

"*Sgt. Pepper* was such an achievement that nothing could possibly follow it." Certainly no subsequent Beatles album had the seismic impact of *Sgt. Pepper*. And the Beatles' psychedelic phase would be over by the end of 1967. Their next project, the *Magical Mystery Tour* album and film, was as out of step as *Sgt. Pepper* was perfectly timed. The film, which had its premiere on BBC television on December 26, tried but failed to capture the lighthearted hippie zeitgeist of the day, and was widely panned.

"The whole boring saga confirmed a long held suspicion of mine that the Beatles are four rather pleasant young men who have made so much money that they can apparently afford to be contemptuous of the public," James Thomas wrote in the *Daily Express*, a view shared by most other critics. It was the first time the Beatles had been so harshly raked over the coals.

Facts and Figures

SGT. PEPPER WAS A COMMERCIAL and critical success straight out of the gate. In the UK, the album was released on June 1, 1967, and it entered the charts at No. 1 in both *Melody Maker* (where it stayed for twenty-two weeks) and the *NME*.

It entered *Record Retailer*'s chart at No. 8, moving to No. 1 the following week (and staying there for a total of twenty-seven weeks), and it topped the chart in *Disc and Music Echo* as well. The album has sold over five million copies in the UK alone. In the US, the album was released on June 2, 1967. It entered the *Billboard* charts at No. 8, then topped the chart the following week (holding the top spot for fifteen weeks). It also topped the charts in *Cash Box* and *Record World*. It has sold over eleven million copies in the US.

Sgt. Pepper would also top the charts in Australia, Canada, Norway, Sweden, and West Germany. And it would go on to win four Grammy awards: Album of the Year, Best Contemporary Album, Best Engineered Album (Non-Classical), and Best Album Cover.

Sgt. Pepper has never been out of print, though the mono edition of the album did go out of print. The next

appearance of *Sgt. Pepper* material came in 1973, with the release of a pair of compilation albums, *1962-1966* and *1967-1970*, which distilled the Beatles' recorded output to four LPs. The following *Sgt. Pepper* songs were included: "Sgt. Pepper's Lonely Hearts Club Band," "With a Little Help from My Friends," "Lucy in the Sky with Diamonds," and "A Day in the Life." It was the first time the latter song was released with a clean intro, not seguing from the "Sgt. Pepper" reprise.

Both sets were very popular; *1967-1970* reached No. 2 in the UK and topped the US charts. In 1976, a new edition was released on blue vinyl (as the album sleeve was bordered in blue). The first CD release came in 1993, when it reached No. 4 in the UK charts, and No. 1 on the *Billboard*'s Top Pop Catalog chart. A remastered edition was released in 2010, and also charted, again reaching No. 4 in the UK, No. 29

on *Billboard*'s Top 200 chart in the US, and again topping the magazine's Catalog Albums chart.

The Beatles: The Collection was released by Mobile Fidelity Sound Lab in 1982, featuring remastered sound. The albums were packaged in new sleeves featuring a picture of a tape box. *The Beatles: Mono Collection* was also released in 1982, featuring every album the Beatles had released in mono.

In 1978, *Sgt. Pepper* was reissued as a picture disc. It was finally released on CD in 1987 (and reissued on vinyl and cassette as well). The dog whistle/run-out groove gibberish was added to the release—the first time these embellishments had appeared since the initial release of the album. All the CDs were combined in *The Beatles Box Set*, released in 1988.

Anthology 2, released in 1996, features a number of *Sgt. Pepper* outtakes. Unfortunately, aside from

RIGHT: The Beatles—and dancers—on the set of the "Hello Goodbye" music video.

BELOW: The 1978 picture disc edition of *Sgt. Pepper*.

the "Sgt. Pepper" reprise, they are newly created composite performances, drawn from various takes—a disappointment if you wanted to chart a song's development. The songs include: "A Day in the Life," "Good Morning Good Morning," "Only a Northern Song," "Mr. Kite!," "Lucy in the Sky with Diamonds," and the instrumental backing track of "Within You Without You." The album topped the charts in the UK and US.

The *Yellow Submarine Songtrack*, released in 1999, marked the first time the *Sgt. Pepper* tracks had been remixed from the original multitrack tapes. The album was released in conjunction with the reissue of the *Yellow Submarine*

film, and included "Sgt. Pepper," "With a Little Help from My Friends," "Lucy in the Sky with Diamonds," "When I'm Sixty-Four," and "Only a Northern Song." The album reached No. 8 in the UK and No. 15 in the US.

The Beatles' catalog was remastered in 2009, the new releases featuring substantially improved sound. The stereo *Sgt. Pepper* was available as a standalone CD (which charted at No. 5 in the UK) and as part of a boxed set (which charted at No. 24 in the UK and No. 15 in the US). At the same time, the mono mix of the album was made available on CD for the very first time, but only as part of the thirteen-disc set *The Beatles in Mono* (which charted at

No. 57 in the UK and No. 40 in the US). A mono vinyl box followed in 2014.

The same year saw the release of the video game *The Beatles: Rock Band*, which breaks the instrumental parts and vocals into individual "stems," a unique way to experience the album. All of the album's tracks were either included with the game or made available as downloads.

In 2015, the *1* and *1+* sets appeared. *1+* is a 1CD/2DVD (or Blu-ray) release, featuring a video shot on the night the band recorded "A Day in the Life." The set also includes the video for "Hello Goodbye"—the only time the Beatles were filmed performing in their vibrant *Sgt. Pepper* suits.

THE LEGACY

149

Musically, they fared better: *Magical Mystery Tour* reached No. 2 in the UK (where it was released as a double EP), and No. 1 in the US (where it was released as a single album featuring the other singles the Beatles had released in 1967). But after donning their colorful *Sgt. Pepper* costumes one more time for the promo film of "Hello Goodbye," the last single the Beatles released in 1967 (which topped the charts on both sides of the Atlantic), all psychedelic paraphernalia was packed

away. It was back to basics, as the thumping piano intro of the band's next single, "Lady Madonna" (released in March 1968), made abundantly clear. The single's flip side, "The Inner Light," also marked the end of an era, being the last of Harrison's Indian-flavored songs released during his Beatles years.

"Lady Madonna" was another No. 1, and so it seemed that despite the *Magical Mystery Tour* hiccup, all was still well in Beatledom. But in fact the

ABOVE: The Beatles en route by coach to the West Country for location work on the *Magical Mystery Tour* film, September 12, 1967.

ABOVE LEFT: Roll up, roll up: a ticket to the *Magical Mystery Tour* fancy-dress party, which took place in London on December 21, 1967.

OPPOSITE: John Lennon's psychedelic Phantom V Rolls Royce, 1967.

.

first crack in the Beatles armor had come before the Summer of Love had faded into autumn, with the death by accidental overdose of Brian Epstein, on August 27, 1967. In future years, Epstein's abilities as a manager would be questioned, particularly in regards to the financial deals he negotiated for the Beatles. And since the band had ceased touring, his day-to-day role in their lives had been diminished. It's also been speculated that when his contract with the Beatles came up for renewal in 1967, the group wouldn't have re-signed with him. But whatever his presumed flaws, Epstein had also provided the organizational base which held the group together.

Lennon, for one, had an ominous feeling about the group's future without their manager. "I knew we were in trouble then," he told *Rolling Stone*. "I didn't really have any misconceptions about our ability to do anything other than play music and I was scared. I thought, 'We've fuckin' had it.'"

> **WHEN WE WERE MAKING IT, I THINK ALL OF US THOUGHT, 'THIS HAS GOT A VERY THIN PLOT. WE HOPE THIS IDEA OF DOING A THING WITHOUT A PLOT WORKS, BECAUSE THE ONE THING WE'RE GONNA BE ABLE TO SAY IS—IT HASN'T GOT A PLOT.'"**
>
> Paul McCartney on *Magical Mystery Tour*

LET US BE

In the wake of Epstein's death, the Beatles began inexorably drifting apart. In the summer of 1967 they'd all traveled to Greece, where they contemplated buying their own island where they could live together communally. One year later, the idea of such camaraderie was a forgotten dream. Lennon had left his wife Cynthia, McCartney had broken up with his longtime girlfriend Jane Asher, and the two had taken up with new partners (artist Yoko Ono and photographer Linda Eastman, respectively). Each man began pursuing his own interests, and the Beatles' main creative force—the two people responsible for writing the majority of the group's songs—was irrevocably split.

Relations between the band members deteriorated to the point that Ringo Starr briefly walked out on the group in August 1968; Harrison would also quit the band temporarily in January 1969.

Yet in public, they continued to maintain a united front. The double album set *The Beatles*, released in 1968, was a strong seller and received generally positive reviews (Tony Palmer in the *Observer* calling Lennon and McCartney "the greatest songwriters since Schubert"), and the accompanying single, the anthemic "Hey Jude," was a worldwide smash. Though their involvement in the *Yellow Submarine* animated film, also released in 1968, was minimal, its commercial success was welcome.

Following the disastrous January 1969 sessions that were supposed to produce a new album and TV special (and during which the Beatles made their final live performance on the roof of their Apple Corps. building on January 30), the band managed to put aside their personal animosities and record *Abbey Road*, widely regarded as one of their best albums. The extended medleys on side two even had a whiff of *Sgt. Pepper* about them, harkening back to a time when the imaginative heights the group could reach in the recording studio knew no bounds.

And then it was over. On April 10, 1970, news outlets around the world broke the story that McCartney had announced he was leaving the Beatles, via a Q&A included with advance copies of his solo debut, *McCartney*, that were sent out to the media, saying the split was due to "personal differences, business differences, but most of all because I have a better time with my family."

The *Let It Be* film and album, salvaged from the January 1969 sessions and compiled with little input from the group, was released soon after, to a generally lackluster reception. (The scenes of the group squabbling with each other are said to be a reason why the film has yet to be released on DVD.) In a sign that they were clearly moving on, Lennon, Harrison, McCartney, and Starr all released solo albums in 1969. The Beatles were now part of history.

ABOVE LEFT: The Beatles' final live performance, an impromptu concert on the roof of Apple Corps., January 30, 1969.

ABOVE: A promotional poster for *Let It Be*.

OPPOSITE: A badge produced in the 1970s makes clear Beatles fans' feelings about the band's continuing absence from the pop world.

> "THERE'S NOT MANY SPECIAL PEOPLE AROUND. . . . IF LENNON/MCCARTNEY ARE SPECIAL, THEN HARRISON AND STARKEY ARE SPECIAL, TOO. WHAT I'M SAYING IS THAT I CAN BE LENNON/MCCARTNEY TOO, BUT I'D RATHER BE HARRISON." George Harrison, 1970

And yet, at the same time, the Beatles never really went away. Certainly for the four now ex-Beatles, questions about their years with the group would factor into every interview they did for the rest of their lives. Meanwhile, as new music trends and fads came and went, the band's musical legacy became the subject of constant reevaluation.

As the seventies rolled on, *Sgt. Pepper* was increasingly described as a period piece, musically as irrelevant as last year's fashions. The very year the group officially split up, Charlie Gillett scrutinized their music in *The Sound of the City* and found *Sgt. Pepper* wanting, writing that it "showed the group at its most removed from the material." He was also dismissive of their later years, saying of the band, "They no longer had anything to say, and amused themselves by seeing how many different ways they could say nothing."

Roy Carr and Tony Tyler's *The Beatles: An Illustrated Record* (1975), the first book to critique every officially released Beatles record, was more charitable, but in the case of *Sgt. Pepper* pushed the music into the background in favor of praising how it had been recorded, calling the album "surely the Beatles' greatest technical achievement and, if hindsight reveals many of the contrivances, they weren't in any way apparent in June 1967, high-water mark of the psychedelic era." The *NME Book of Rock*, published in 1975, called it "a patchy, inconsistent album," while conceding it featured the "most important song the band ever recorded": "A Day in the Life."

This was an observation that would become increasingly common: dismissing *Sgt. Pepper*'s psychedelic fantasy element while acknowledging the power that the album's final track still exuded.

Two further occurrences during the decade helped fuel a rising *Sgt. Pepper* backlash. The first was punk, a genre whose players desired to get back to the exhilarating, primitive rawness of fifties rock 'n' roll, wiping out the over-produced dinosaurs who had diluted rock's original power in the process. In their bracing song "1977" (the B-side to "White Riot"), the Clash famously declared that Elvis, the Beatles, and the Stones were old news. (The line echoed Jimi Hendrix's denouncement of earlier musical fads when he stated that surf music was over in "Third Stone from the Sun" in 1967.)

Punk had no need for *Sgt. Pepper*'s bag of tricks; no ADT or backward cymbals, let alone symphony orchestras. Even so, something of a grudging respect for the music remained; the Damned put a cover of the Beatles' "Help!" on the B-side of their 1976 single "New Rose," while Siouxsie and the Banshees recorded "Helter Skelter" for their 1978 debut album *The Scream*.

More damaging to the album's legend was the disappointing *Sgt. Pepper's Lonely Hearts Club Band* movie, released in 1978. The film was produced by Robert Stigwood, then riding high on the success of his back-to-back hits *Saturday Night Fever* and *Grease*, both of which spun off film soundtracks that sold in the millions. However, *Sgt. Pepper* was hampered by a limp script that was essentially a rehash of *Yellow Submarine*, with the Lonely Hearts Club Band (the Bee Gees), headed up by Billy Shears (Peter Frampton), enlisted to save the town of Heartland from falling into decline and decay.

The film received scathing reviews. "This isn't a movie, it's a business deal set to music," Janet Maslin wrote in the *New York Times*. "The movie may have been conceived in a spirit of merriment, but watching it feels like playing shuffleboard at the absolute insistence of a bossy shipboard social director. When whimsy gets to be this overbearing, it simply isn't whimsy any more." With a $20 million gross, *Sgt. Pepper* at least recouped its $13 million budget, but that figure was miniscule

compared to the sums earned by *Saturday Night Fever* ($237 million) and *Grease* ($380 million).

The film's soundtrack (produced by George Martin), reached a lowly No. 38 in the UK; in the US, it reached No. 5 and was certified platinum (amid stories of many more millions of preordered copies being returned to the record company). Earth, Wind & Fire's cover of "Got to Get You into My Life" fared the best on the charts, reaching the Top 10 in the US and topping the R&B chart.

" LET'S HOPE CLONES AREN'T LIKE THIS. FROM THE SONG SELECTION, YOU WOULDN'T EVEN KNOW THE ORIGINALS WERE ONCE A ROCK AND ROLL BAND. MOST OF THE ARRANGEMENTS ARE LIFTED WHOLE WITHOUT BENEFIT OF VOCAL PRESENCE . . . OR RHYTHMIC INTEGRITY." *Village Voice* critic Robert Christgau on the *Sgt. Pepper* soundtrack

Robin Gibb and Aerosmith had more modest successes with "Oh! Darling" and "Come Together," respectively. ("Within You Without You" and "Lovely Rita" were the only *Sgt. Pepper* songs not featured on the soundtrack.)

The critical beating of the original album continued. In *Stranded: Rock and Roll for a Desert Island* (1979), edited by Greil Marcus, twenty critics wrote about the one album they'd take with them to the titular island. *Sgt. Pepper* was conspicuously missing from the roster, but its lingering reputation was such that the matter of its absence still had to be addressed. Marcus regarded it as an album that had outlived its usefulness, one "which today seems artificial where *Rubber Soul* still seems full of life" and went on to dismiss it as "a Day-Glo tombstone for its time." It was a view shared by critic Lester Bangs, who, in 1980, noted that the garage-rock classic "Louie Louie" had "already lasted longer than *Sgt. Pepper*."

THE LEGACY

Cover Me

"YESTERDAY" IS THE BEATLES SONG that's generated the most cover versions; over 3,000, according to the *Guinness Book of World Records*. But numerous artists have covered *Sgt. Pepper*'s songs—and sometimes the entire album—over the years as well, while the album's cover is likely the most parodied piece of record art in rock history.

The first person to do a cover of a *Sgt. Pepper* song was Jimi Hendrix, who performed the title track just three days after the album's official UK release on June 4 at London's Saville Theatre. Hendrix never recorded a studio version of the track, but live versions have appeared on his numerous posthumous releases.

The first album widely regarded as being highly influenced by *Sgt. Pepper*, if not a direct cover, was the Rolling Stones' dip into psychedelia, *Their Satanic Majesties Request*, released in December 1967. Even the album's cover was taken by the same photographer who shot *Sgt. Pepper*'s cover, Michael Cooper. As John Lennon noted when speaking to *Rolling Stone* magazine in 1970, "I'd like to just *list* what we did and what the Stones did two months after, on every *fuckin'* album and every *fuckin'* thing we did, Mick does *exactly* the same. He imitates us . . . *Satanic*

Majesties is *Pepper*." Keith Richards appeared to agree, when he talked about *Sgt. Pepper* to *Esquire* in 2015: "Some people think it's a genius album, but I think it's a mishmash of rubbish, kind of like *Satanic Majesties*—'Oh, if you can make a load of shit, so can we.'"

The first proper parody of the cover art would have been the Mothers of Invention's *We're Only in It for the Money*, released in 1968. A collage was prepared for the album's front cover, though the people are hard to recognize, given that many of them have a black bar across their eyes. Robert H. Jackson's Pulitzer Prize-winning photo of Lee Harvey Oswald is one of the most recognizable images; Jimi Hendrix, who dropped by the studio when the cover shot was being taken, stands at the far right.

Mothers leader Frank Zappa asked Paul McCartney for permission to parody the cover. McCartney said it was

fine with him, but that the record company might have an objection, and to run it by them. According to his memoir, *Many Years from Now*, McCartney himself contacted EMI and gave his consent. There are varying accounts as to what happened next; *Many Years from Now* says that Zappa's record company, Verve, didn't want to approach EMI, while in other versions it was Capitol that had an objection to the image. So on initial release, the image appeared on the inner gatefold, though it was reinstated as the cover on later editions. The album parodied *Sgt. Pepper*'s back cover art as well, and featured a sheet of cutouts, in emulation of the sheet that had been included in the Beatles' album.

Instead of covering a single song, some artists have ambitiously taken on the whole album. *Sgt. Pepper Knew My Father*, released in the UK in 1988, was a charity compilation that featured the

> "*SGT. PEPPER* WAS OKAY, BUT . . . I GOT THE IMPRESSION FROM WHAT WAS GOING ON AT THE TIME THAT THEY WERE ONLY IN IT FOR THE MONEY—AND THAT WAS A PRETTY UNPOPULAR VIEW TO HOLD." Frank Zappa, 1988

ABOVE LEFT: A signed copy of *The Rutles* (1978), an album of tongue-in-cheek Beatles pastiches.

ABOVE MIDDLE: The *Sgt. Pepper*-like 3D cover of the Rolling Stones' 1967 LP *Their Satanic Majesties Request.*

ABOVE RIGHT: Frank Zappa (*left*) and his Mothers of Invention visit Big Ben, London, September 1967.

likes of Sonic Youth ("Within You Without You"), the Wedding Present ("Getting Better"), and the Fall ("A Day in the Life"). A single released from the album, "With a Little Help from My Friends" by Wet Wet Wet, backed with "She's Leaving Home" by Billy Bragg and Cara Tivey, topped the UK charts.

Mojo Presents Sgt. Pepper: With a Little Help from His Friends, released in the UK in 2007, was a free giveaway included with issues of the magazine. The artists are all alternative-rock musicians. The best known, Echo and the Bunnymen, don't even cover a *Sgt. Pepper* song, they perform "All You Need Is Love." Other acts include Simple Kid ("Sgt. Pepper"), the M's ("Good Morning Good Morning"), and Dave Cloud and

the Gospel of Power ("Lovely Rita").

Cheap Trick released their live performance of the album in its entirety, *Sgt. Pepper Live*, in 2009 on CD and DVD. They were an appropriate band to tackle the album, given their previous Beatles covers ("Day Tripper," "Magical Mystery Tour"); their 1980 album *All Shook Up* was produced by George Martin. The band's guitarist, Rick Nielsen, and drummer, Bun E. Carlos, also performed on John Lennon and Yoko Ono's comeback album, *Double Fantasy* (1980), on early versions of the tracks "I'm Losing You" and "I'm Moving On." Their versions weren't used on the final album, though "I'm Losing You" did later appear on the *John Lennon Anthology.*

THE LEGACY

LEFT: Wayne Coyne of the Flaming Lips onstage at Barclays Center, New York, February 5, 2014.

Other artists who have recorded *Sgt. Pepper* in its entirety include the Andy Timmons Band, who issued the instrumental *Plays Sgt. Pepper* in 2011, and Big Daddy, whose *Sgt. Pepper's* from the same year has the band performing the songs in different styles: "Lucy in the Sky with Diamonds" as it would sound if Jerry Lee Lewis was performing it, for example. Canada's Art of Time Ensemble, featuring members of Barenaked Ladies and Toad the Wet Sprocket, released a fun version of the album in 2013; a year later, the Flaming Lips issued *With a Little Help from My Fwends*, a track-for-track remake of the album featuring collaborations with Miley Cyrus, Moby, and My Morning

Jacket, among others. Finally, the 2006 bootleg *Sgt. Petsound's Lonely Hearts Club Band*, by the "Bleachles," is a mash-up of *Sgt. Pepper* and the Beach Boys' *Pet Sounds*. Though it's an idea with a lot of potential, the end result is a disappointment, as the songs aren't meshed together terribly well, and led to a cease-and-desist order from EMI.

Among the parodies of the artwork, Rhino's *Golden Throats* series deserves a mention. The first volume, *The Great Celebrity Sing Off* (1988), parodies *Sgt. Pepper's* cover art, and includes William Shatner's unhinged version of "Lucy in the Sky with Diamonds." The sequel, *Golden Throats 2* (1991), parodies the *Satanic Majesties* cover art. The fourth

in the series, *Celebrities Butcher Songs of the Beatles* (1997) parodies the Beatles' "Butcher Cover" (the controversial original artwork for *Yesterday and Today*, showing the band members draped in pieces of meat and body parts of plastic dolls), and contains George Burns's rendition of "With a Little Help from My Friends" and Shatner's "Lucy." The Simpsons' *The Yellow Album* (1998) has a great *Sgt. Pepper* parody cover with inside jokes Beatles fans will appreciate: on the original, a doll on the right wears a sweater reading "Welcome the Rolling Stones"; on the Simpsons' cover, a Krusty the Clown doll wears a shirt reading "Welcome Ren and Stimpy."

"Who in the hell does any songs from that album anymore?" Bangs asked. "Yet, a few years ago, some people were saying *Sgt. Pepper* will endure a hundred years."

It's a debate that continues to this day. In a July 1967 *Village Voice* article, Richard Goldstein had predicted, "When the Beatles' work as a whole is viewed in retrospect, it will be *Rubber Soul* and *Revolver* which stand as their major contributions." It was a prescient observation, especially as the latter album was concerned; over the years, *Revolver* would rise higher and higher in the numerous "best-of" lists that would come to dominate magazines and internet websites. But *Sgt. Pepper* managed to maintain its hold in both the hearts and minds of the public, and occasionally the critics, as well, placing respectably in, if not topping, its own share of said listings.

YESTERDAY AND TODAY

If Brian Epstein's death had been the catalyst for the Beatles' breakup, it was another death that would—at least symbolically—help bring the group back together. The shocking murder of John Lennon on December 8, 1980— less than a month after the release of the comeback album he'd recorded with his wife Yoko Ono, *Double Fantasy*— seemed to slam the door on the sunny optimism of the 1960s with a grim finality. Now the Beatles really were confined to history, with no chance of a real reunion. In the cold light of the new decade, the colorful *Sgt. Pepper* era in particular took on an increasingly nostalgic hue.

Prior to Lennon's death, there were only a handful of books on the group worthy of serious consideration. Now there was an explosion of new offerings, from gossipy tell-all accounts (*The Love You Make: An Insider's Story of the Beatles* by Peter Brown, one of Epstein's aides), to memoirs (*Beatle! The Pete Best Story* by the band's drummer prior to Ringo Starr), to reference books (Kevin Howlett's *The Beatles at the BEEB*, a tie-in with the radio program of the same name). Lennon was deified in Ray Coleman's *John Winston Lennon* and *John Ono Lennon*, and denounced in Albert Goldman's *The Lives of John Lennon*.

On the serious end of the spectrum was Philip Norman's *Shout! The Beatles in Their Generation*, the first full biography of the group since Hunter Davies' *The Beatles: The Authorized Biography* (1968), and the first of Mark Lewisohn's remarkable Beatles histories, *The Beatles Live!* and *The Beatles Recording Sessions*.

And developing technologies would soon have a new way of bringing the group's music to the public. The compact disc was introduced in 1982, and record companies quickly realized there was easy money to be made by reissuing their back catalogs in the new format. The Beatles catalog wouldn't appear on CD for a few more years. But there was an anniversary coming up later in the decade that would prove to be irresistible.

What more perfect time could there be to reintroduce *Sgt. Pepper*, whose opening line was "It was twenty years ago today" than on the very date— June 1, 1987—when it would ring with a new accuracy? The album's release on CD was celebrated with a private party held at the locale where the record had been created, now renamed Abbey Road Studios. McCartney was the sole Beatle on hand at the event, receiving what was said to be the world's first platinum CD award, and having the honor of cutting the first slice from a giant cake decorated like the drum on the *Sgt. Pepper* cover.

While the release of the first seven Beatles albums on CD had been covered in the media, the release of *Sgt. Pepper* generated far more media excitement; "probably the most hectic Beatles promotional activity ever," Mark Lewisohn wrote in his monthly news column for the revived *Beatles Monthly Book*. (The fan magazine had ceased publication in December 1969, but was restarted in May 1976, and continued publishing until January 2003.) Along with coverage in major magazines, and radio specials, Granada Television in the UK produced the excellent two-hour documentary *It Was Twenty Years Ago Today*, accompanied by a tie-in book of the same name, written by Derek Taylor, who'd worked as the Beatles' publicist.

The documentary and book placed the album in its context, covering not just the making of *Sgt. Pepper*, but also the events of 1967 itself—"the rosy high point of the sixties," as the book's cover put it. The hippies and flower children of that year had now reached middle age, and as they looked back at the golden period of their youth, some increasingly regarded the era through rose-tinted spectacles, as when Ian MacDonald proclaimed with some jubilance, "Anyone unlucky enough not to have been aged between fourteen and thirty during 1966–1967 will never know the excitement of those years in popular culture," in *Revolution in the Head*, his trenchant examination of the Beatles' music.

ABOVE: Ringo Starr, Paul McCartney, George Harrison, and George Martin, reunited at Abbey Road to promote the first release from the Beatles' *Anthology* series.

OPPOSITE: McCartney at the Playhouse Theatre, London, July 27, 1989.

> "MY MODEL FOR BUSINESS IS THE BEATLES: THEY WERE FOUR GUYS THAT KEPT EACH OTHERS' NEGATIVE TENDENCIES IN CHECK; THEY BALANCED EACH OTHER. AND THE TOTAL WAS GREATER THAN THE SUM OF THE PARTS." Apple founder Steve Jobs

Conversely, Charles Shaar Murray, in his review of the album for *Q*, understood that not everyone was equally bedazzled by the era, pointing out that *Sgt. Pepper* "has been both hailed as rock's definitive masterpiece and attacked as the incarnation of the moment when the music went off the rails almost for good." But while regarding *Sgt. Pepper* as something of a period piece, "an album immovably fixed in time, as 'dated' a record as anything in pop," he also underscored its historical importance: "The sheer sonic ingenuity deployed on these sessions taught everybody, for better or worse, to hear music differently. . . . Like it or not, it was the record which changed the rules."

From this point on, the former Beatles began to more willingly embrace their past. When McCartney and Harrison toured in the seventies, they were eager to establish themselves as solo artists, putting only a handful of Beatles songs in their sets. Now, when they returned to live performance, Beatles numbers began to dominate, particularly in McCartney's case. After a ten-year gap in touring, McCartney began to breathe new life into *Sgt. Pepper*, performing the title song on his 1989–1990 tour, and since then tackling most of the album's other songs as well: all the numbers on which he sang live (excepting "When I'm Sixty-Four"), one on which he didn't ("Being for the Benefit of Mr. Kite!"), and even creating a medley of "A Day in the Life" with "Give Peace a Chance."

Another media frenzy surrounded the release of *The Beatles Anthology* documentary series, which aired on television in November 1995, and the accompanying double CD sets, released in 1995 and 1996 (the companion book

All You Need Is *Love*

THE CIRQUE DU SOLEIL'S *LOVE* is a wonderfully imaginative show that reworks the Beatles' music to stunning effect. Coupled with the troupe's athletic acrobatics, *Love* is an inventive production that draws on the strengths of these two creative forces. As Yoko Ono put it in the show's tenth-anniversary program, "The Beatles were like acrobats of the mind, and Cirque du Soleil are acrobats of the body. So when they come together, it makes something that's whole."

The Cirque du Soleil ("Circus of the Sun") troupe staged its first shows under that name in Quebec in 1984. Since then, the Cirque has expanded substantially, with numerous companies touring different shows around the world, and, in 2016, six different shows running in Las Vegas (including *Love*). The shows typically have a basic narrative, a story told through dance and acrobatics, embellished by colorful costumes and live music.

George Harrison was a big fan of the company and, being an ex-Beatle, was able to meet one of Cirque's founders, Guy Laliberté. In 2000, Harrison suggested that the Cirque should produce a Beatles show. Laliberté agreed, and Paul McCartney, Ringo Starr, and Ono (representing John Lennon's estate) came on board as well. Sadly, Harrison would die of cancer on November 29, 2001, so he would not see the end result of the wheels he'd set in

motion. (His estate is now represented by his wife, Olivia.)

The biggest challenge was how to handle the music. At that time, most Cirque shows used live music. But Neil Aspinall, the Beatles' longtime friend and roadie who went on to become the head of Apple Corps., insisted that the band's own music should be used. In order to make the show more modern dance-oriented, an idea was floated to rework the music along the lines of the recent JXL remix of Elvis Presley's "A Little Less Conversation," which had been a worldwide hit in 2002. But Aspinall was wary of having a third party take on such a venture, so he tapped Beatles producer George Martin for the job.

Martin was happy to be involved, but his hearing had become severely compromised over the years, so he brought in his son, Giles Martin, to coproduce with him. "We wanted to do

something that sounded natural," Giles told me in 2006. "And our first approach was thinking, 'Let's do something so the Beatles sound like they're playing in the room. Let's see if we can recreate that same feeling that we get when we put a multitrack on the tape and press play in the studio and you hear that intimacy, you hear that feel.'"

The first track Giles tackled was "Tomorrow Never Knows," which he mashed up with "Within You Without You." The underlying drone of each song makes them a good choice for a mash up, but Giles recalled that his father's reaction wasn't initially positive: "He was thinking, 'Well, this probably isn't a very good idea; they're not going to like this.' And then it was funny, Paul and Ringo came in, and Olivia and Yoko, and they heard it, and that's what they liked—they liked that edgier thing. And then the rule book was thrown out the window." The show's beginning illustrates how

ABOVE LEFT: A program for the Beatles' *Love*.

ABOVE RIGHT: A nighttime view of the Las Vegas Strip, with a *Love* billboard prominent on the skyline.

much fun the Martins were able to have in creating the score. After "Because," which is heard a cappella (heightening the beautiful vocal harmonies), comes the final chord of "A Day in the Life"—played backward. That segues into the opening chord of "A Hard Day's Night," then Starr's drum solo from "The End," and finally "Get Back"; it's a pulse-pounding moment made even more exciting as *Love*'s dancers explode into action. There are naturally a number of Beatles hits in *Love*—"I Want to Hold Your Hand," "Yesterday," "Something"—but the Martins were also interested in getting less well-known numbers into the show, a mash-up of "Drive My Car," "The Word," and "What You're Doing" being a good example.

The storyline is loosely based on the Beatles' own story, recreating the post–World War II era, the arrival of Beatlemania, the psychedelic age (a *Sgt. Pepper* figure is seen throughout the

show), and the political turmoil of the late 1960s. There are no characters playing the Beatles, though their images are projected on screens. "Hey Jude" closes the show—it inevitably ends in a sing-along—followed by another sing-along during the encore, "All You Need Is Love," during which confetti falls on the audience.

Love opened on June 30, 2006, at the Mirage casino and hotel in Las Vegas, in the theater previously used for Siegfried and Roy's magic show, which featured rare white tigers and white lions. The space was redesigned so that Love is presented in the round; each seat is equipped with its own speakers. For the tenth anniversary, the show was revamped, with new dance sequences, a few song changes, and a lot of technological improvements.

McCartney, Starr, and Ono all attended the tenth-anniversary performance on July 14, 2016.

The Love soundtrack, released in 2006, came in two different packages: a single-CD edition and a CD/DVD set with a 5.1 surround sound mix. It reached no. 3 in the UK and no. 4 in the US, and went on to win two Grammys for Best Compilation Soundtrack for Motion Picture, Television, or Other Visual Media, and Best Surround Sound Album. A DVD documentary, The Beatles Love: All Together Now (2008), also won a Grammy for Best Long Form Music Video.

Love is especially enjoyable if you know the Beatles' catalog inside out; it's fun to see how the different elements of the songs have been taken apart and put back together.

ABOVE: Two stills from a preview performance of Love at the Mirage hotel and casino, Las Vegas, June 27, 2006.

ABOVE: Talk show host Larry King, Paul McCartney, Yoko Ono, Olivia Harrison, Ringo Starr, and Cirque du Soleil founder Guy Laliberté attend *Love*'s first anniversary show, June 26, 2007.

"I CAN SEE THIS GOING ON FOR ANOTHER CENTURY OR SOMETHING. THE BEATLES' MUSIC IS GROWING, WHICH IS REALLY NICE." Yoko Ono at *Love*'s tenth-anniversary show

IT HAD TO BE JUST RIGHT. WE TRIED AND I THINK SUCCEEDED IN ACHIEVING WHAT WE SET OUT TO DO. IF WE HADN'T THEN IT WOULDN'T BE OUT NOW." John Lennon on *Sgt. Pepper*, 1967

was a few years in coming; it was finally published in 2000). It was the first time since they'd been jointly interviewed for Hunter Davies's authorized biography in the sixties that McCartney, Harrison, and Starr sat down to tell the entire story of the band. (Lennon's contributions to the project were taken from the voluminous archive of interviews he'd done over the years.) It was decidedly subjective, but all the more intriguing because of that. Though they made a concerted effort to skirt areas of potential controversy—the arguments that broke out during the January 1969 *Let It Be* sessions were played down, for example—they were also far more open than in most other interviews. The *Anthology* book in particular provides much detail about every aspect of the band's career, from the perspective of the very musicians who had lived through it.

The *Anthology* documentary opens with a telling sequence: a tight close up of the Beatles' logo on Starr's drums, the camera pulling back to reveal the Beatles playing the song "Help!"; then, as the camera continues to pull back, the group receding into the distance, the sound of their music drowned out by the screams of their fans, the words "The Beatles Anthology" towering above

them, as if they're being dwarfed by their own image. But it was nonetheless an image they continued to burnish. The "Threetles," as they were dubbed by the media, even endeavored to create "new" Beatles songs for the *Anthology*, taking two Lennon demos they'd been given by Yoko Ono and adding their own voices and instruments to the tracks. The elaborate video for "Free as a Bird" offered a condensed Beatles history, filled with references to their different songs; "Real Love" was largely a collection of film clips from the archives, interspersed with footage of the Threetles working on the track. The shots of the one time Fab Four, now men in their fifties, provided a poignant reminder of the passage of time. It was the last major Beatles project the three would work on. Harrison died of lung cancer in 2001, making the *Anthology* their final important statement on what it meant to be a Beatle.

Though falling in and out of favor over the years—"in and out of style," as the album's title track might put it—*Sgt. Pepper* has retained its position as the key jewel in the Beatles' crown. No other Beatles album has prompted so much discussion or debate, from the moment of its release to present day. For every

writer like the *Guardian*'s Richard Smith, who slammed the record as "the most overrated album of all time" on *Sgt. Pepper*'s fortieth anniversary in 2007, there are those who are quick to counter such views, as in *Rolling Stone*'s 2012 "500 Greatest Albums of All Time" list, which hailed *Sgt. Pepper* as "the most important rock & roll album ever made, an unsurpassed adventure in concept, sound, songwriting, cover art and studio technology by the greatest rock & roll group of all time."

In histories of the band, *Sgt. Pepper* is rightly seen as the centerpiece of the Beatles' story. It was the last album the band created before they began to fragment. It was an album of songs that sparkled, songs that tickled the imagination in the way no other Beatles songs had done before, or would again. *Sgt. Pepper* opened the door to new musical possibilities, without any sense of exclusivity; the listener was invited to join in, not simply observe. Beyond the fine songs, *Sgt. Pepper* encouraged people to look at the rock album, and rock music itself, in a new and different way. Popular music would never be the same again.

Though Lennon never hesitated to criticize his own work (saying of

SGT. PEPPER AT FIFTY

ABOVE: The Beatles celebrate the launch of *Sgt. Pepper* in Brian Epstein's front room, May 19, 1967.

"A Day in the Life," less than a year after recording the song, "It's still not half as nice as I thought it was when we were doing it"), he also recognized that *Sgt. Pepper* was "a peak" for the band. And Derek Taylor, in his *Twenty Years Ago Today* book, accurately pinpointed the album's timeless appeal: "Paul McCartney says today that other Beatles albums outsold it, George Harrison is not at all sure it was their best LP, and I remember Ringo saying years ago that he preferred *Abbey Road*. But out of the twelve of their basic *oeuvre* it is still *Sgt. Pepper* that speaks loudest of its era."

On *Revolver*'s closing track, Lennon had urged the listener to listen to the color of their dreams. On *Sgt. Pepper*, the Beatles took their own advice, creating a bold, vivid album that still holds true to its promise: a splendid time is guaranteed for all.

Bibliography

Anthony, Gene. *Summer of Love: Haight-Ashbury at Its Highest*. San Francisco: Celestial Arts, 1980.

Badman, Keith. *The Beatles Off the Record: Outrageous Opinions and Unrehearsed Interviews*. New York: Omnibus Press, 2000.

Beatles, The. *The Beatles Anthology*. San Francisco: Chronicle Books, 2000.

Boyd, Pattie. *Wonderful Today: The Autobiography*. London: Headline, 2007.

Carlin, Peter Ames. *Catch a Wave: The Rise, Fall, and Redemption of the Beach Boys' Brian Wilson*. Emmaus, PA: Rodale Books, 2006.

Carr, Roy, and Tyler, Tony. *The Beatles: An Illustrated Record*. New York: Harmony Books, 1975.

Décharné, Max. *Kings Road: The Rise and Fall of the Hippest Street in the World*. London: Weidenfeld & Nicolson, 2005.

Du Noyer, Paul. *Conversations with McCartney*. New York: Overlook Press, 2016.

Emerick, Geoff, and Massey, Howard. *Here, There and Everywhere: My Life Recording the Music of the Beatles*. New York: Gotham Books, 2006.

Green, Jonathon (ed.). *Days in the Life: Voices from the English Underground, 1961–71*. London: William Heinemann Ltd., 1988.

Giuliano, Geoffrey. *Blackbird: The Life and Times of Paul McCartney*. New York: Dutton, 1991.

Harrison, George. *I, Me, Mine*. London: Genesis, 1980.

Heylin, Clinton. *The Act You've Known for All These Years: A Year in the Life of Sgt. Pepper and Friends*. New York: Canongate, 2007.

Kehew, Brian, and Ryan, Kevin. *Recording the Beatles*. Houston, TX: Curvebender Publishing, 2006.

Lewisohn, Mark. *The Beatles Recording Sessions: The Official Abbey Road Studio Sessions Notes 1962–1970*. New York: Harmony Books, 1988.

Lewisohn, Mark. *The Complete Beatles Chronicle*. New York: Harmony Books, 1992.

MacDonald, Ian. *Revolution in the Head: The Beatles' Records and the Sixties*. Chicago: Chicago Review Press, 2005.

Martin, George, with Pearson, William. *With a Little Help from My Friends: The Making of Sgt. Pepper*. New York: Little, Brown & Co., 1994.

McDermott, John, with Kramer, Eddie. *Hendrix: Setting the Record Straight*. New York: Warner Books, 1992.

Miles, Barry. *Paul McCartney: Many Years from Now*. New York: Owl Books, 1998.

Miles, Barry. *The Beatles Diary Volume 1: The Beatles Years*. New York: Omnibus Press, 2001.

Miles, Barry. *In the Sixties*. London: Pimlico, 2003.

Miles, Barry. *London Calling: A Countercultural History of London Since 1945*. London: Atlantic Books, 2011.

Nicholson, Stuart, *Jazz-Rock: A History*. London: Canongate, 1998.

Norman, Philip. *Shout! The Beatles in Their Generation*. New York: Fireside, 2003.

Nuttal, Jeff. *Bomb Culture*. London: MacGibbon and Kee, 1968.

Shankar, Ravi. *Raga Mala: The Autobiography of Ravi Shankar*. New York: Element Books, 1999.

Sheff, David. *All We Are Saying: The Last Major Interview with John Lennon and Yoko Ono*. New York: St. Martin's Griffin, 2000.

Sounes, Howard. Fab: *An Intimate Life of Paul McCartney*. Philadelphia, PA: Da Capo Press, 2010.

Southall, Brian. *Abbey Road: The Story of the World's Most Famous Recording Studios*. London: Patrick Stephens, 1982.

Spizer, Bruce, and Daniels, Frank. *Beatles for Sale on Parlophone Records*. New Orleans: 498 Productions, 2011.

Taylor, Derek. *It Was Twenty Years Ago Today: An Anniversary Celebration of 1967*. New York: Fireside, 1987.

Turner, Steve. *A Hard Day's Write: The Stories Behind Every Beatles Song*. London: Carlton Books, 2012.

Wenner, Jann S. *Lennon Remembers*. New York: Verso 2000.

Winn, John C. *That Magic Feeling: The Beatles' Recorded Legacy Volume Two, 1966–1970*. New York: Three Rivers Press, 2009.

This book contains references to the historical use of LSD ("acid") in several places. Readers should be aware that the use of LSD is illegal in the US and Canada, and throughout the rest of the world. LSD is a dangerous substance. The authors, publishers, and Elephant Book Company are in no way condoning or encouraging its use by referring to it in these pages.

Endnotes

12 "One reason we ..." Andy Gray, *Hit Parader*, May 1967

14 "What this gang ..." Jo Durden-Smith, *So Far Out It's Straight Down*, Granada Television, January 18, 1967

15 "People are very ..." Norrie Drummond, *NME*, May 27, 1967

18 "The thing about ..." Dave Sholin, RKO Radio Network, December 8, 1980

20 "When the recording ..." Stuart Dredge, *Guardian*, September 26, 2012

21 "By 1961 in Liverpool ..." Nicholson, *Jazz-Rock*

26 "an older drummer ..." *The Beatles Anthology*

27 "about the only ..." Jann S. Wenner, *Rolling Stone*, November 15, 2007

31 "There were some ..." Green (ed.), *Days in the Life*

41 "At this concert ..." Miles, *In the Sixties*

45 "distorted, hypnotic drum ..." Lewisohn, *The Beatles Recording Sessions*

57 "New recording techniques ..." *Arena: Produced by George Martin*, BBC4, March 9, 2016

62 "We were fed ..." Miles, *Paul McCartney*

65 "I was originally ..." *The Beatles Anthology*

65 "Ravi had written ..." Shankar, *Raga Mala*

66 "That was a pretty ..." Taylor, *It Was Twenty Years Ago Today*

66 "It had to ..." Norrie Drummond, *New Musical Express*, May 27, 1967

66 "One's ears are ..." Aubrey Beardsley, "The Art of the Hoarding," *The New Review*, July 1894

68 "We created a ..." *Mojo*, March 2007

69 "We were dealing ..." Décharné, Kings Road

69 "Kids were already ..." *The Beatles Anthology*

69 "We thought, 'Let's ... '" Miles, *Paul McCartney*

70 "I did a lot of ..." Miles, *London Calling*

71 "The Fool were ..." *The Beatles Anthology*

71 "They hadn't somehow ..." Giuliano, *Blackbird*

71 "I was so ..." Heather Harris, *Paraphilia Magazine*, August 23, 2012

72 "I spent many ..." Badman, *The Beatles Off the Record*

73 "It made absolute ..." Taylor, *It Was Twenty Years Ago Today*

73 "I remember staring ..." *The Beatles Anthology*

75 "one of the greatest ..." *The Beatles Anthology*

75 "little suburban house" Miles, *Paul McCartney*

78 "I Remember Robert ..." Mark Ellen, *Saga*, May 2012

80 "Who would my ..." *The Beatles Anthology*

80 "John wanted Hitler ..." *The Beatles Anthology*

80 "The boy who ..." Peter Blake, *Mojo*, March 2007

83 "I talked to ..." Charlotte Higgins, *Guardian*, June 3, 2004

83 "They wanted to ..." *Mojo*, March 2007

86 "People think they're ..." *The Beatles Anthology*

86 "We had a drink ..." Peter Blake, *Mojo*, March 2007

86 "Robert said, 'No ...'" Du Noyer, *Conversations with McCartney*

87 "I told them ..." Southall, *Abbey Road*

87 "One of the things ..." Miles, *Paul McCartney*

90 "It wasn't practical ..." Taylor, *It Was Twenty Years Ago Today*

90 "One of the ideas ..." Southall, *Abbey Road*

91 "It was the most ..." *The Beatles Anthology*

93 "The sky, the palm ..." Taylor, *It Was Twenty Years Ago Today*

93 "Sgt. Pepper was ..." *The Beatles Anthology*

93 "The album was a ..." *The Beatles Anthology*

96 "You just have to ..." Norrie Drummond, *NME*, May 27, 1967

99 "With any kind ..." Miles, *International Times*, November 1966

100 "thinking it could ..." Sounes, *Fab*

102 "It was completely ..." Martin, *With a Little Help from My Friends*

103 "It's part fact ..." Alan Aldridge, *Observer Magazine*, November 1967

105 "arted it up ..." Miles, *Paul McCartney*

105 "Strawberry Fields is ..." David Sheff, *Playboy*, January 1981

106 "We always liked ..." Miles, *Paul McCartney*

108 "I was imagining ..." Miles, *Paul McCartney*

108 "He was a bit ..." Norrie Drummond, *NME*, May 27, 1967

110 "It was about ..." Miles, *Paul McCartney*

110 "a sound building ..." Norman, *Shout!*

115 "Suddenly, on the plane ..." *The Beatles Anthology*

115 "We could say ..." Miles, *Paul McCartney*

117 "A psychedelically painted ..." Nicole Rudnik, *Paris Review*, June 11, 2012

119 "That was our ..." Joan Goodman, *Playboy*, December 1984

119 "shoved the mics ..." Lewisohn, *The Beatles Recording Sessions*

121 "*Sgt. Pepper* is called ..." David Sheff, *Playboy*, January 1981

121 "all those pissy ..." Miles, *Paul McCartney*

121 "a weak track ..." Emerick, *Here, There and Everywhere*

121 "I wasn't very ..." Davies, *The Beatles*

123 "was the image ..." David Sheff, *Playboy*, January 1981

124 "The greatest rock ..." Carlin, *Catch a Wave*

125 "People are saying ..." Sounes, *Fab*

125 "You don't have ..." Miles, *Paul McCartney*

126 "We did the whole ..." Badman, *The Beatles Off the Record*

127 "That's the important ..." Miles, *Paul McCartney*

127 "I was a hitter" David Sheff, *Playboy*, January 1981

127 "The way [the piano] ..." Miles, *Paul McCartney*

129 "The song was ..." Harrison, *I Me Mine*

129 "Suddenly we had ..." Martin, *With a Little Help from My Friends*

131 "an unnecessary surfeit ..." Emerick, *Here, There and Everywhere*

132 "This record will ..." *NME*, May 20, 1967

134 "I played chess ..." *Blender*, March 2008

136 "They made funny ..." Lewisohn, *The Beatles Recording Sessions*

136 "I just listened ..." *Rolling Stone*, August 27, 1987

137 "Sgt. Pepper's Lonely ..." Martin, *With a Little Help From My Friends*

137 "On Sgt. Pepper" Kehew and Ryan, *Recording the Beatles*

140 "See, I never ..." Elliot Mintz, *Inner-View*, August 29, 1977

140 "I remembered the ..." Martin, *With a Little Help from My Friends*

140 "I totally, literally ..." Sounes, *Fab*

140 "The music blasted ..." Taylor, *It Was Twenty Years Ago Today*

144 "That was like ..." McDermott with Kramer, *Hendrix*

144 "We had been ..." Andy Gray, *NME*, July 22, 1967

151 "When we were ..." David Frost, BBC TV, December 27, 1967

155 "There's not many ..." Howard Smith, WABC-FM New York, May 1, 1970

156 "Let's hope clones ..." Robert Christgau, *Village Voice*, September 4, 1978

159 "*Sgt. Pepper* was ..." Kurt Loder, *Rolling Stone*, July 14, 1988

160 "It's in the realm ..." Arun Rath, *All Things Considered*, NPR, October 25, 2014

161 "It was just ..." Jonathan Ross, *The Jonathan Ross Show*, ITV, December 8, 2014

163 "My model for ..." Steve Kroft, *60 Minutes*, CBS, 2003

167 "I can see ..." Steve Appleford, *Rolling Stone*, July 15, 2016

168 "It had to be ..." Norrie Drummond, *NME*, May 27, 1967

Picture credits

p2: Mark Naboshek; p7: Mark Naboshek (photographed by Robert Greeson); p8: Bettmann/Getty Images; p9: TL, BL, Mark Naboshek; R, Redferns/GAB Archive/Getty Images; p11: Rolls Press/Popperfoto/Getty Images; p12: L, Mark and Colleen Hayward/Getty Images; R, Michael Ochs Archives/Getty Images; p13: L, Michael Ochs Archives/Getty Images; R, Bettmann/Getty Images; p14: L, Rolls Press/Popperfoto/Getty Images; R, PYMCA/Chris Morris/REX/Shutterstock; p16: Rolls Press/Popperfoto/Getty Images; p19: L, Hulton Archive/William Lovelace/Getty Images; R, Photoquest/Getty Images; p20: Terry O'Neill/REX/Shutterstock;

p21: L, Popperfoto; R, Mark and Colleen Hayward/Getty Images; p22: L, Michael Ochs Archives/Getty Images; R, Rolls Press/Popperfoto/Getty Images; p23: L, Bruce Fleming/REX/Shutterstock; R, Topfoto; p24: L, Hulton Archive/Central Press/Getty Images; R, Redferns/John Hoppy Hopkins/Getty Images; p25: Sipa Press/REX/Shutterstock; p27: L, Blank Archives; C, Redferns/Cummings Archives/Getty Images; R, Michael Ochs Archives/Getty Images; p28: TL, © 1960 Estate of J. V. L. Hopkins; TR, © Ted Streshinsky/CORBIS/Corbis via Getty Images; BR, International Times; p30: © Ted Streshinsky/CORBIS/Corbis via Getty Images; p31: Fred W. McDarrah/Getty Images; p33: L, Paul Popper/Popperfoto/Getty Images; R, Bettmann/Getty Images; p34: Bettmann/Getty Images; p36: Popperfoto/Getty Images; p37: L, R, © 1965 Estate of J. V. L. Hopkins;

p38: L, Dudley Edwards; R, Associated News/REX/Shutterstock; p39: L, International Times; R, McInnerney Archive; p40: L, Popperfoto/Getty Images; p41: L, George Freston/Getty Images; R, Evening Standard/Getty Images; p42: R. McPhedran/Express/Getty Images; p43: L, The Print Collector/Getty Images; C, public domain; R, M&N/Alamy; p44: Bob Gill; p45: L, Kaye/Express/Getty Images; Martin Cook via Dudley Edwards; p46: Dudley Edwards; p48: Graham Keen/Pictorial Press Ltd./Alamy; p49, p50: McInnerney Archive; p51: Daily Mail/REX/Shutterstock; p52: William N. Jacobellis/New York Post Archives / (c) NYP Holdings, Inc. via Getty Images; p53: L, Estate Of Keith Morris/Redferns/Getty Images; R, Wolfgang Kunz/ullstein bild via Getty Images; p54: L, Blank Archives/Getty Images; R, Baron Wolman/Iconic Images/Getty Images; p55: International Times;

p56: L, Evening News/REX/Shutterstock; R, George Stroud/Express/Getty Images; p57: © 1966 Estate of J. V. L. Hopkins; p58: International Times; p59: John Williams/BIPs/Getty Images; p60: REX/Shutterstock; p63: TL, Popperfoto/Getty Images; TR, Rolls Press/Popperfoto/Getty Images; B, Keystone-France/Gamma-Keystone via Getty Images; p65: TL, Bettmann/Getty Images; TR, Trinity Mirror/Mirrorpix/Alamy; BL, © LFI/Roy Cummings/Photoshot; BR, Clive Limpkin/Express/Getty Images; p66: L, David Graves/REX/Shutterstock; R, © 1966 Estate of J. V. L. Hopkins; p67: Ian Tyas/Keystone/Getty Images; p68: L, Rolls Press/Popperfoto/Getty Images; R, Hulton Archive/Getty Images; p69: International Times; p70: L, Sylvan Mason/REX/Shutterstock; R, Bill Zygmant/REX/Shutterstock; p71: L, Pictorial Press Ltd/Alamy; R, Trinity Mirror/Mirrorpix/Alamy; p73: TL, George Hurrell/Columbia/REX/Shutterstock; C, Archive Photos/Getty Images; BR, Underwood Archives/REX/Shutterstock; p74: TL, CA/Redferns/Getty Images; TC, Moviestore Collection/REX/Shutterstock; TR, Associated Newspapers/REX/Shutterstock; BL, Jack Orren Turner/Library of Congress; BC, Bettmann/Getty Images; BR, Douglas Glass/Paul Popper/Popperfoto/Getty Images; p75: TL, Rolls Press/Popperfoto/Getty Images; TC, Hulton Archive/Keystone/Getty Images; TR, Universal History Archive/UIG via Getty Images; BL, Baron/Getty Images; BR, Hulton Archive/Getty Images; p76: TL, Colorsport/REX/Shutterstock; TC, Victor Blackman/Express/Getty Images; TR, Moviestore Collection/REX/Shutterstock; BL, Juergen Vollmer/Redferns/Getty Images; BR, Haywood Magee/Getty Images; p77: L, HeritageAuctions/Bournemouth/REX/Shutterstock; R, Jann Haworth; p79: TL, Ken Harding/BIPs/Getty Images; TR, Fred Mott/Evening Standard/Getty Images; B, Chris Morphet/Redferns/Getty Images; p80: L, Associated Newspapers/REX/Shutterstock; R, Local World/REX/Shutterstock; p81: L, R, Tony Evans/Getty Images; p82: TL, Alain Le Garsmeur/Corbis via Getty Images; BL, BR, Rockaway Records (www.rockaway.com); p85: L, Jann Haworth; R, © National Pictures/Topfoto; p86: L, Masatoshi Okauchi/REX/Shutterstock; R, Nils Jorgensen/REX/Shutterstock; p87: L, David Lodge/FilmMagic/Getty Images; C, Mike Lawn/REX/Shutterstock; R, Masatoshi Okauchi/REX/Shutterstock; p89: T, Mark Naboshek (photographed by Robert Greeson); B, Jeff Goode/Toronto Star via Getty Images; p90: L, Roy Jones/Evening Standard/Getty Images; R, Moviestore Collection/Alamy; p91: L Michael Ochs Archives/Getty Images; R, Mark Naboshek (photographed by Robert Greeson); p92: L, © Jann Haworth, photographed by Richard Severy; R, Mark Naboshek; p93: L, Gephardt Daily/Jamie Cowen; R, © PA Photos/Topfoto; p94: Mark and Colleen Hayward/Getty Images; p97: TL, John Frost Historical Newspapers; C, Bettmann/Getty Images; BL, Mark Naboshek; BR, Mark Naboshek (photographed by Robert Greeson); p98: L, Larry Ellis/Express/Hulton Archive/Getty Images; Daily Mail/REX/Shutterstock; p99: Mark Waugh/Alamy; p101: The Times/Frank Herrmann/News Syndication; p103: L, Matt Cetti-Roberts/LNP/REX/Shutterstock; R, razorpix/Alamy; p104: Pictorial Press Ltd./Alamy; p105: Tracks/Alamy; p106: REX/Shutterstock; p107: George Clerk/istockphoto; p109: L, Trinity Mirror/Mirrorpix/Alamy; R, Nils Jorgensen/REX/Shutterstock; p111: L, R, Tracks Images; p112: Larry Ellis/Express/Hulton Archive/Getty Images; p114: Trinity Mirror/Mirrorpix/Alamy; p115: REX/Shutterstock; p117: L, R, Dudley Edwards; p118: Dudley Edwards; p120: Associated Newspapers/REX/Shutterstock; p123: Associated Press/Topfoto; p125: L, CBW/Alamy; R, Erich Auerbach/Getty Images; p126: Photograph by Frank Herrmann, Camera Press London; p127: Mark and Colleen Hayward/Getty Images; p128: L, Peter Brooker/REX/Shutterstock; R, Tracks Images/Alamy; p131: L, GAB Archive/Getty Images; R, Jason Bye/Alamy; p132: Mirrorpix; p133: L, Bettmann/Getty Images; R, Sydney O'Meara/Evening Standard/Hulton Archive/Getty Images; p135: L, Express Newspapers/Getty Images; R, David Magnus/REX/Shutterstock; p136: Keystone USA/REX/Shutterstock; p138: Laurence Griffiths/Getty Images; p141: L, Bernard Howden/Fotolibria; R, International Times; p142: L, John Pratt/Keystone/Getty Images; R, Tracks Images; p143: International Times; p144: David Magnus/REX/Shutterstock; p145: L, R, David Magnus/REX/Shutterstock; p146: L, R, Pictorial Press Ltd./Alamy; p147: L, R, Photos12/Alamy; p149: L, Mark Naboshek; R, Keystone USA/Alamy; p150: T, Tracks Images; C, Potter/Express/Getty Images; p151: Bill Zygmant/REX/Shutterstock; p152: L, John Frost Historical Newspapers; R, Evening Standard/Getty Images; p153: L, Wallace/Daily Mail/REX/Shutterstock; R; Hulton Archive/Getty Images; p154: L, Express Newspapers/Getty Images; R, Moviepix/Getty Images; p155: David J. & Janice L. Frent/Corbis via Getty Images; p156: Ron Galella/WireImage/Getty Images; p157: Everett Collection/REX/Shutterstock; p159: L, Mark Naboshek (photographed by Robert Greeson); C, CBW/Alamy; R, Pictorial Press Ltd./Alamy; p160: Kevin Mazur/Getty Images for CBGB; p162: Reuters/Alamy; p163: Rob Verhorst/Redferns/Getty Images; p165: T, tobiasjo/istockphoto; BL, Mark Naboshek (photographed by Robert Greeson); p166: L, Stuart Kelly/Alamy; R, Ethan Miller/Getty Images; p167: Ethan Miller/Getty Images; p169: John Downing/Getty Images.

Index

Authors and acknowledgments

Mike McInnerney was an active member of the counterculture in London during the sixties. His psychedelic posters, painted murals, and work for alternative journals helped promote the music, arts, politics, and events of the era. Following a stint as art editor of the *International Times*, he designed record sleeves including the Who's *Tommy* and produced editorial illustration work for leading journals such as the *Sunday Times* and *Nova* magazine. His work is exhibited at major institutions around the world, including London's Whitechapel Art Gallery and Victoria and Albert Museum, and the Whitney Museum, New York.

Bill DeMain is a writer and musician based in Nashville. He has written for publications including *MOJO*, *Classic Rock*, *Musician*, *Entertainment Weekly*, *Mental Floss*, and *Performing Songwriter*. He's also contributed essays to several books, including *The Beatles: Ten Years That Shook the World*, *The History of Rock*, *The MOJO Collection*, and more.

Gillian G. Gaar has written for numerous publications including *Mojo*, *Rolling Stone*, and *Goldmine*. Her previous books include *She's a Rebel: The History of Women in Rock & Roll*, *Entertain Us: The Rise of Nirvana*, *100 Things Beatles Fans Should Know and Do Before They Die*, and *Return of the King: Elvis Presley's Great Comeback*. The first Beatle she saw in concert was Paul McCartney at the Kingdome, June 10, 1976. She lives in Seattle.

Spencer Leigh was born and still lives in Liverpool, England, and is an acknowledged authority on the Beatles. He has been broadcasting his weekly show *On the Beat* on BBC Radio Merseyside since 1985, and has written more than twenty-five books, including biographies of Simon & Garfunkel and Frank Sinatra, and several volumes on the Beatles.

Dudley Edwards is a British artist who first rose to prominence during the Summer of Love. As cofounder, with Douglas Binder and David Vaughan, of the design firm BEV, he painted murals, designed furniture and light shows, and customized cars for musicians including the Beatles, the Who, and Jimi Hendrix. Since then, he has worked with everyone from Yves St. Laurent to the Saudi Arabian Ministry of Defense, and has taught and exhibited around the world.

Acknowledgments

The editors would like to thank the following people for their help with this book: Sally Claxton, Martin Cook, Bill DeMain, Dudley Edwards, Gillian G. Gaar, Bob Gill, Robert Greeson, Jann Haworth, Alex Johnstone, Spencer Leigh, Mike McInnerney, Mark Naboshek, Paul Palmer-Edwards, and Ellie Wilson.

Editorial credits

Editorial Director: Will Steeds
Concept and Project Editor: Tom Seabrook
Picture Researcher: Sally Claxton